From the Iliad to the Odyssey: A Retelling in Prose of Quintus of Smyrna's Posthomerica

David Bruce

Published by David Bruce, 2022.

FROM THE ILIAD TO THE ODYSSEY: A RETELLING IN PROSE OF QUINTUS OF SMYRNA'S POSTHOMERICA

First edition. July 7, 2022.

Copyright © 2022 David Bruce.

ISBN: 979-8201997250

Written by David Bruce.

Table of Contents

Educate Yourself
Read Like A Wolf Eats
Be Excellent to Each Other
Books Then, Books Now, Books Forever

In this retelling, as in all my retellings, I have tried to make the work of literature accessible to modern readers who may lack the knowledge about mythology, religion, and history that the literary work's contemporary audience had.

Do you know a language other than English? If you do, I give you permission to translate this book, copyright your translation, publish or self-publish it, and keep all the royalties for yourself. (Do give me credit, of course, for the original retelling.)

I would like to see my retellings of classic literature used in schools, so I give permission to the country of Finland (and all other countries) to give copies of any or all of my retellings to all students forever. I also give permission to the state of Texas (and all other states) to give copies of any or all of my retellings to all students forever. I also give permission to all teachers to give copies of any or all of my retellings to all students forever. Of course, libraries are welcome to use my eBooks for free.

Teachers need not actually teach my retellings. Teachers are welcome to give students copies of my eBooks as background material. For example, if they are teaching Homer's *Iliad* and *Odyssey*, teachers are welcome to give students copies of my *Virgil's* Aeneid: *A Retelling in Prose* and tell them, "Here's another ancient epic you may want to read in your spare time."

A Note

Homer created the epic poems the *Iliad* and the *Odyssey*. The *Iliad* tells only a small part of the story of the Trojan War. For example, the *Iliad* does not tell the story of the Trojan Horse although Homer knew about the Trojan Horse and assumed that his audience knew its story. Other, shorter epic poems that made up the Epic Cycle told the rest of the story of the Trojan War.

The *Iliad* and the *Odyssey* show many signs of oral composition; they were written down perhaps in the eighth century B.C.E. The *Iliad* and the *Odyssey* have survived to the present time, but the other epic poems of the Epic Cycle have been lost. Quintus of Smyrna, writing perhaps in the third century C.E., wrote an epic poem that retold the tales recounted in the lost epic poems of the Epic Cycle. He told the story of the Trojan War from the burial of Hector until the Greeks set sail for home after the fall of Troy. In other words, he told the story of the Trojan War from the end of the *Iliad* to when Odysseus sets sail for home in the *Odyssey* after Troy has fallen. Homer is an epic poet of genius; Quintus of Smyrna is not. Quintus of Smyrna, however, did a service to Humankind by retelling the stories of the other epic poems of the Epic Cycle and telling us some of the most important stories, such as those about the deaths of Achilles and of Paris and the fall of Troy, that Homer did not tell us. Unfortunately, he chose not to tell the story of the theft of the Palladium from Troy by Odysseus and Diomedes; he merely mentions that story.

In this retelling, as in all my retellings, I have tried to make the work of literature accessible to modern readers who may lack the knowledge about mythology, religion, and history that the literary work's contemporary audience had.

Since so many hundreds of years lie between Homer and Quintus of Smyrna, we should not be surprised that some inconsistencies appear in their work. For example, according to Homer, Paris and Apollo kill Achilles. According to Quintus of Smyrna, only Apollo kills Achilles. Another example: According to Homer, Achilles goes to the Land of the Dead, which he hates. According to Quintus of Smyrna, Achilles becomes a god and lives on an island that Poseidon gives to him. The people living near Achilles worship him.

Chapter 1: The Story of Penthesilea

After the funeral of Hector, the Trojans stayed behind their walls. They were afraid to fight the Greeks now that Achilles had ended his anger at Agamemnon. As long as Achilles had been angry at Agamemnon, he had stayed away from war and had not fought. Now he was fighting again in war.

The Trojans were like a herd of cattle that refuses to face a lion and instead runs away from its fangs and claws. The Trojans knew all too well how many brave warriors Achilles had killed at the Scamander River and before the walls of Troy. They remembered how Achilles had killed Hector and dragged his corpse around Troy. They remembered the many cities allied to Troy that Achilles had conquered both by land and by sea. They remembered how many warriors Achilles had killed ever since he had first arrived at Troy with the other Greeks. The grieving Trojans had good reason to stay behind the walls of their city.

But new allies arrived for the Trojans from the land of the warrior women known as the Amazons, who lived by the river Thermodon in northeast Asia Minor. The Amazon warrior-queen Penthesilea, whose father was Ares, the god of war, arrived with twelve other Amazons to fight in the Trojan War. She had good reasons for wanting to fight in the war. First, she wanted to win glory as a warrior. Second, she wanted to avoid criticism at home. Penthesilea had accidentally killed Hippolyta, her sister: While hunting, Penthesilea had thrown a spear at a stag but missed the stag and hit Hippolyta. Third, she hoped to appease the Furies with deeds of glory and with sacrifices. The Furies — who are invisible to all except the guilty — wreak vengeance when someone kills a member of his or her family.

Penthesilea brought these twelve Amazons with her: Alcibie, Antandre, Antibrote, Bremousa, Clonie, Derimacheia, Derinoe, Evandre, Hippothoe, Harmothoe, Polemousa, and Thermodosa. Penthesilea was the best and the most glorious of the Amazons. Penthesilea outshone the other Amazons just as the Moon outshines the stars, and just as the goddess Dawn outshines the Horae: the goddesses of the seasons.

When Penthesilea and the other warrior-women arrived at Troy, the Trojan citizens marveled at them. Penthesilea's beauty impressed them but also troubled them: She was a beautiful woman, but she was also a warrior who was willing to kill and to be killed in battle. She smiled, and her eyes sparkled, and she blushed occasionally out of modesty, yet she was willing to thrust a spear into a man's belly and then pull it and the warrior's intestines out.

Troy needed allies to fight for it, and the Trojan citizens looked at Penthesilea and her Amazons the way that a farmer whose crops have long been suffering from drought looks at a rainstorm above his fields.

Even the sorrow of Priam, king of Troy, lessened when he saw Penthesilea and her Amazons. Many of Priam's citizens — and many of his sons — had died in battle. Most recently, his son Hector, a hero and the strongest warrior of Troy, had died. Priam was like a man who had been blind and wished to die if he could not see again. A doctor or a god partially restores his sight, and he rejoices to see again, although his eyes still ache.

Priam welcomed Penthesilea and her Amazons into his palace and showed them every sign of respect available in Troy after ten years of siege by the Greeks. He treated Penthesilea as if she were a daughter who had undertaken dangerous travel and returned home after twenty years of absence. Priam ordered his servants to prepare for the Amazons a meal of the best food available. He also gave Penthesilea wonderful presents and promised her many more if she succeeded in helping the Trojans defeat the Greeks.

Penthesilea made no ordinary vows: She vowed to kill Achilles, to defeat the Greek army, and to burn the Greek ships. These vows were impressive, but foolish, because she did not realize the strength and skill of Achilles in battle.

Andromache, the widow of Hector, heard Penthesilea make these vows. Knowing the might of Achilles, Andromache thought to herself about the overconfident Penthesilea, *You vow to do much more than you can accomplish. Achilles is much more dangerous than you know — he will kill you, and quickly. You must be fated to die at Troy. My strong husband, Hector, was much better at fighting in battles than you are, but his strength did not save him — Achilles killed him. Yet Hector was like a god! I wish that I had not lived to see the day when Achilles speared my husband in the neck. I wish that I had not lived to see the day when Achilles dragged the corpse of my husband around the walls of Troy. Achilles made me a widow, and each day I cry for Hector.*

Night arrived, and servants made a bed for Penthesilea. Athena, who supported the Greeks in the Trojan War, sent a lying dream to her to make her eager for a battle that she would not win. In the dream, Ares, her father, appeared before her and urged her to fight Achilles face to face. The dream delighted Penthesilea, who believed that it prophesied that she would kill the best warrior of the Greeks, but this dream, like all too many dreams, deceived.

When dawn arrived, Penthesilea armed herself with the gifts of Ares, her father: golden greaves to protect her legs, a breastplate, a sword in a silver and ivory scabbard, a gleaming shield shaped like a half-moon with curved horns, and a helmet with plumes. Fully dressed in armor, Penthesilea resembled one of the thunderbolts that Zeus uses as a weapon. She also armed herself with two javelins and a double-bladed battle-ax. The battle-ax was a gift to her from Eris, the goddess who values strife and discord. Penthesilea rejoiced in this gift.

Although the Trojan warriors had previously wanted to avoid fighting Achilles, who killed every enemy he met in battle, Penthesilea persuaded the Trojan warriors to go again into battle.

Penthesilea herself was eager to fight. She rode a swift horse that Oreithyia, wife of the North wind, gave to her when she visited Thrace. This horse was faster than the Harpies, who are like birds but with the heads of women.

Penthesilea rode to war with the other Amazons and the Trojan warriors. Fate made her go to her death on her first and last day of battle in the Trojan War. She stood out among the other warriors like Athena stands out when she goes to fight giants or like Eris stands out when she runs among warriors and creates havoc. The Trojans followed her like sheep following a ram, the leader of the flock.

Priam raised his hands to the temple of Zeus, king of gods and men, and prayed, "May Penthesilea, the daughter of the god of war, have success in battle and kill many Greek warriors. May Penthesilea return safely home from the battle. Zeus, keep her safe because she is the daughter of your son Ares and because she is your granddaughter. Keep her safe for my sake because I have suffered so much from the deaths of many of my sons in battle. Help us Trojans. A few of the descendants of Dardanus, who is your son and my father and the former king of Troy, are still alive. Show mercy to us and allow Troy to remain unconquered."

In answer to Priam's prayer, Zeus sent an omen. An eagle cried out on Priam's left, and Priam looked at it. It was clutching a dying dove in its talons. Priam grieved because the left side is the unlucky, sinister side. This omen was negative. Priam believed that he would never see Penthesilea return from battle safely.

The Greek warriors watched the Amazons and the Trojan warriors approach. The Trojans were like wild animals that prey on sheep. Penthesilea was like a fire that destroys everything in its path.

The Greek warriors said among themselves, "For a long time, the Trojans would not fight after Achilles killed Hector. Someone has roused their fighting spirit although we thought that they would stay behind the walls of Troy. It almost seems as if a god has convinced the Trojans to fight. We will fight them with courage and skill — we also have gods on our side."

The Greek warriors armed themselves and came from their ships and camps to fight their enemy. The two armies clashed, and the ground reddened.

The Amazons found success and defeat in battle.

Penthesilea killed Molion, Persinous, Elissus, Antitheus, Lernus, Hippalmus, Haemonides, and Elasippus.

The Amazon Derinoe killed Laogonus.

The Amazon Clonie killed Menippus, who had come to Troy with Protesilaus, the first Greek to be killed in the Trojan War. Cycnus had killed Protesilaus when the Greeks landed on the Trojan shore at the start of the war, and then Achilles had killed Cycnus.

Angry at the death of Menippus, the Greek Podarces speared Clonie in the stomach. Blood gushed from the wound, and her intestines were visible.

Penthesilea retaliated by deeply cutting Podarces' right arm. Blood gushed as he ran from her. He ran only a little way, and his fellow warriors grieved for him as he died.

Idomeneus, king of Crete, killed the Amazon Bremousa with a spear by her right breast. She fell like a mountain tree harvested by woodcutters. The tree makes a whistling sound as it falls, and Bremousa wailed as she fell.

Meriones, the aide of Idomeneus, killed the Amazons Evandre and Thermodosa. He killed one with a spear to the head and the other with a sword between her hips.

Little Ajax killed the Amazon Derinoe with a spear through her collarbone.

Diomedes killed the Amazons Alcibie and Derimacheia, using his swords to cut off their heads at the shoulders. A man can kill heifers quickly with an ax to their necks. Alcibie and Derimacheia fell quickly to the ground, and their heads lay far from their shoulders.

Sthenelus killed the Trojan Cabeirus, who had traveled from Sestus, a town on the Hellespont, to fight in the war, and he would never return alive to his home.

Angry at the death of Cabeirus, Paris, who had taken Helen from Menelaus, aimed an arrow at Sthenelus, who was not fated to die at that time. The arrow instead hit the Greek Evenor, who was fated to die.

Angry at the death of Evenor, the Greek Meges acted as if he were a lion in the midst of sheep. Enemy warriors were afraid of him as he killed the Trojans Itymoneus and Agelaus, who fought under the command of the Trojan allies Nastes and Amphimachus. Meges also killed many other enemy warriors with his spear. The goddess Athena had blessed Meges with courage.

The Greek Polypoetes killed the Trojan Dresaeus, whose parents were Theiodamas and Neaera, who had slept together under the snow-capped mountain Sipylus, where Niobe had been turned to stone. Niobe was guilty of the sin of pride. She had seven sons and seven daughters, and she boasted that she was more worthy of praise than the goddess Leto, who had only one son and one daughter. It is not wise to place yourself above a god or goddess, and Leto's children — Apollo and Artemis — killed all fourteen of Niobe's children. Apollo killed all of Niobe's sons, and Artemis killed all of Niobe's daughters. Niobe mourned the deaths of her children, and even after Zeus turned her to stone, she still mourns the deaths of her children — tears can be seen trickling down her stone cheeks. From a distance, the stone looks like Niobe. Up close, the stone looks like a cliff and a spur of the mountain.

The battle continued, and deaths occurred frequently. Trojans and Greeks died, and as they died, they groaned.

Penthesilea continued to fight; she stayed strong and energetic. She was like a lioness that attacks cattle. The Greek warriors were surprised at her endurance, and they retreated from her. She followed them the way that storms and huge waves follow ships that try to speed away from danger.

Penthesilea shouted, "All of you Greeks will pay for making war upon Troy and Priam! None of you Greeks will escape me! None of you will live to be a blessing to your aged parents and to your wives and children! None of you Greeks will have a tomb; instead, you will be food for dogs and birds! Where are Achilles and Great Ajax? They are your best warriors, so why aren't they fighting? Are they afraid that I will kill them in battle?"

Penthesilea was proud, and she was confident, and she was skilled in war, and she killed many warriors. She cut with her battle-ax, and she inflicted wounds with her javelins. Her horse carried her bow and arrows, and she wore a sword. Fighting with her were mighty Trojans, the friends and brothers of Hector. Spears filled the air and killed Greek warriors, who fell like dying leaves or drops of rain. The ground was wet with blood and covered with corpses. Wounded horses and warriors screamed and died. The Trojans on their horses trampled the dead and the dying Greeks as if they were threshing grain.

Penthesilea impressed the Trojans. As she fought the Greeks, she was like a storm raging against ships on the sea.

One Trojan — his hopes raised too high — said to others, "Clearly, Penthesilea is one of the immortal goddesses. Clearly, Zeus is on our side. Zeus is remembering that Priam is one of his descendants. Penthesilea cannot be mortal. She must be the virgin warrior goddess Athena or Enyo, the goddess of war. Or she may be Eris, goddess of strife, or Artemis, the huntress daughter of Leto. I predict that on this day she will conquer the Greeks and burn their ships — those ships on which they arrived from across the sea to try to conquer Troy, kill our men, and make our women and children slaves. I predict that because of Penthesilea, the Greeks will never return alive to their homes."

So the Trojan spoke, but he too was overconfident. The two best warriors of the Greeks — Great Ajax and Achilles — were not yet fighting in the battle because they were mourning at the burial mound of Patroclus, Achilles' best friend, whom Hector had killed. Achilles had avenged Patroclus' death by killing Hector.

Penthesilea continued to gain glory by killing warriors while Great Ajax and Achilles were not fighting. Her spear killed men by wounding them in the back when they ran away from her, and her spear killed men by wounding them in the front when they ran toward her to fight her. Penthesilea was splattered with blood that was not her own, and she did not grow tired but continued to make enemy warriors spill their blood. Although now Penthesilea was winning glory in battle for herself, soon Achilles would win glory for himself by killing Penthesilea.

A heifer can get into a garden and busily destroy plants. Penthesilea had gotten onto the battlefield and busily destroyed men.

The Trojan women watched the battle, and they were impressed by the glorious deeds of Penthesilea the Amazon. Tisiphone, the daughter of Amphimachus and the wife of Meneptolemus, was especially impressed. She urged the other Trojan women, "Our men fight bravely for our city and our children, so why shouldn't we also fight? In what relevant way are women different from men? We have courage like men. We have eyes and legs and arms like men. We see with the same sunlight, and we breathe the same air. We eat the same food. Why shouldn't we women also fight in battle? Look at Penthesilea, a woman who is superior to so many men who have much experience at making war. She is not fighting for her own city or for her own family, but she is fighting fiercely. Why shouldn't we fight fiercely for our city and our families? We have experienced the deaths of fathers and brothers and husbands and sons. They died fighting for us so that we do not become slaves. So let us also fight. It is better to die in battle than to become a slave. If our men die and Troy falls, our children will also become slaves."

The Trojan women were ready to go to war. They were like bees that have been in their hive all winter and now are eager to leave their hive and go out into warm weather. The Trojan women were ready to stop weaving and to start fighting with cruel weapons.

The Trojan women would have died on the battlefield if Theano, an older woman who was a priestess of Athena, had not reasoned with them.

Theano pointed out, "We have no training in wielding weapons or in waging war. We have no experience in killing men. We lack the strength of the Greek men who will fight us, and we lack the many years of experience in making war that the Greek warriors have. The Amazons are much different from us. From the day they are born, they take pleasure in battle and riding horses. From the day they are born, they do the things that men do. They get training and experience, and so they are always ready to wage war. Their training and experience give the Amazons courage and strong bodies. Penthesilea is much different from us. She is either the daughter of Ares, god of war, or she is herself a goddess come to help us in this war. Either way, she is not like us. Human beings, whether male or female, have their humanity in common, but people are trained to do different tasks, and people ought to do the task for which they are trained. Our men are trained in waging war; we are trained at weaving. Let the men do the work for which they are trained, and let us do the work for which we are trained. Right now, we women have no necessity of going to war. Our warriors are fighting well and are killing many Greek warriors. Let us stay out of the battle."

Theano persuaded the Trojan women to stay behind the walls of Troy. Many of the Trojan women watched the battle from the walls.

Penthesilea was still fighting well and killing many men. The Greek warriors were afraid of her the way that goats are afraid of a leopard. The Greek warriors thought of flight, not fight. They fled; some dropped their armor so they could flee faster. Making the battlefield even more chaotic were horses pulling chariots that no longer had charioteers. The Amazons and the Trojans felt joy in battle; the Greeks felt terror. Penthesilea was like a terrible storm that uproots huge trees as she destroyed Greek warriors.

Penthesilea drove the Greeks back to their ships, and Great Ajax and Achilles heard the sounds of the battle.

Great Ajax said to Achilles, "We are needed in the battle. It grows close, and our ships are in danger of being burned. Both of us have Zeus as an ancestor, and we ought to live up to such a heritage by defending our fellow warriors and our ships. Heracles also had Zeus as an ancestor, and with fewer warriors than we have now he conquered the city of Troy back when Laomedon, the father of Priam, was its king. Your father, Peleus, and my father, Telamon, fought with Heracles and helped conquer Troy. Laomedon had cheated Heracles out of the horses that he had earned by saving the life of Hesione, Laomedon's daughter, and our fathers helped Heracles, the greatest hero of all time, conquer Troy. We need to live up to our fathers, and we need to conquer Troy."

Great Ajax and Achilles armed themselves and went to the battle. Athena blessed both of them with strength.

Seeing Great Ajax and Achilles ready to fight, the Greek warriors rejoiced. Great Ajax and Achilles looked like the two sons of the giant Aloeus: Otus and Ephialtes. These two giants made war against the gods and attempted to carry away goddesses to make them their wives. Otus wanted to marry Artemis, and Ephialtes wanted to marry Hera. Part of their plan was to pile the mountains Ossa and Pelion on top of Mount Olympus.

Great Ajax and Achilles fought and killed many warriors. They were like two lions that kill sheep and drink their blood and eat their flesh. Great Ajax killed Deiochus, Hyllus, Eurynomus, and Enyeus. Achilles killed all of the remaining Amazons except for Penthesilea: Antandre, Antibrote, Harmothoe, Hippothoe and Polemousa. Fighting together, Great Ajax and Achilles easily pushed back the warriors fighting against them. They were like a raging fire destroying the trees of a forest.

Unafraid, Penthesilea advanced toward Great Ajax and Achilles, who were like hunters awaiting a leopard. Great Ajax and Achilles lifted their spears and held them, ready to throw them when necessary.

Penthesilea threw her javelin first. It broke as it hit Achilles' shield, which had been made by the skilled blacksmith god Hephaestus. Such gifts of the gods are not easily pierced.

Penthesilea held her other javelin in throwing position and said, "My first throw was not effective, but I think my next throw will kill. You two warriors are the best of the Greeks, and I want to kill both of you and make this war less burdensome for the Trojans. Come closer and find out how dangerous I am. My father is not mortal; my father is Ares, the god of war. Because of my father, I am more effective in battle than men."

Her words were proud and confident, but both Great Ajax and Achilles laughed.

Penthesilea threw her javelin at Great Ajax, but it hit his greave and did no damage.

Penthesilea groaned, dismayed that neither of her javelins had inflicted any damage.

Great Ajax was an experienced warrior, and he knew the fighting strength of Achilles. He was able to look at Penthesilea, evaluate her fighting strength, and know that Achilles could easily kill her the way that a hawk kills a dove. Great Ajax did not fight Penthesilea; he left and fought Trojans.

Achilles said to Penthesilea, "You are a proud woman, but you cannot live up to your words. Great Ajax and I are the best warriors of the Greeks and indeed the best warriors of the Trojan War. We trace our descent from Zeus himself. Hector himself was afraid to meet us, and I killed him with a spear. You are threatening us, but you will not be able to kill us. You are the one who will die, and your father, Ares, cannot save your life. You will die like a deer hunted by a lion. You should have heard by now of the many warriors I killed while I was fighting by the river that mortals call the Scamander and the immortals call the Xanthus. I threw their corpses into the river and choked it. If you have heard about those many deaths I caused, you should know not to boast about killing me."

Achilles then swiftly attacked, and he speared Penthesilea above her right breast with the spear that Chiron the Centaur had given to Peleus, Achilles' father, who had given it to him. No one other than Achilles was strong enough to wield this spear.

Penthesilea bled and grew weaker. She dropped her battle-ax. She began to lose her eyesight, and she felt agonizing pain. She recovered, a little, and looked at Achilles coming toward her and wondered whether she should draw her sword and defend herself or dismount from her horse and supplicate him, offering him masses of bronze and gold if he would not kill her. Perhaps Achilles would respect her youth — he was also young — and she could continue to live.

But Achilles ran to her quickly and with his spear he pierced both Penthesilea's horse and her body the way that a man pierces pieces of meat on a spit for cooking or the way that a hunter throws a spear that goes through the belly of a deer and then strikes the trunk of a tree.

Both Penthesilea and her horse fell. She lay facedown, and both she and her horse quivered. Penthesilea had fallen the way that a tree falls when a fierce wind topples it.

The Trojans, seeing Penthesilea fall, ran in terror and grief back to their city. Sailors can battle to stay alive on the sea after their ship sinks. Land finally appears, and a few exhausted sailors make it to safety. A few Trojans made it safely back to Troy as they mourned for the loss of Penthesilea and her Amazons and for the loss of so many of their warriors in battle.

Achilles laughed as he stood over the fallen Penthesilea. He said, "Lie there and die, girl. Your corpse will feed dogs and birds. Why did you come here to fight? Were you tricked with bribes? You must have thought that you would return victorious from the battle and return to your home with many valuable gifts from Priam, but the gods did not give you victory in battle. Great Ajax and I are the best of the warriors here. The Greeks value us; the Trojans fear us. You should been a weaver, not a warrior; war takes away the courage even of strong men."

Achilles pulled his spear out of the bodies of Penthesilea and her horse, and then he removed Penthesilea's shining helmet. She was dead, but she was still beautiful. The Greeks gathered around her and marveled at her beauty as she lay on the ground in her armor. She resembled a sleeping Artemis, tired after a long day of hunting lions. Aphrodite, the wife of Ares, had given Penthesilea the gift of beauty, and Achilles regretted that he had killed her. Greek warriors looked at her, and they prayed to the gods that someday they could sleep by a wife as beautiful as Penthesilea. Achilles wished that he had made Penthesilea his bride and taken her home with him to Greece.

Ares grieved at the death of his daughter; the Gales, daughters of the North wind, had brought him the news. He wanted to avenge his daughter by slaughtering Achilles, and he jumped up and sped to Mount Ida like one of Zeus' thunderbolts that shakes Olympus.

But Ares' father, Zeus, was watching. Zeus did not want gods to fight at that time in the wars of men, and so Zeus threw thunderbolts at the feet of Ares to warn him to stay away from the battlefield. Ares recognized the wishes of Zeus, and he stopped his descent the way that a boulder breaks free from a cliff and rolls downward and crushes everything in its path until it reaches level ground and then stops. Zeus is more powerful than any other god. All Olympians must wrench their wills to match the will of Zeus or endure painful punishments. Although Ares grieved over the death of his daughter, he fought against his desire to kill Achilles before the time Achilles was fated to die and he returned to Olympus. Ares knew that Zeus had allowed many of his own sons, including Sarpedon, to die at Troy, and so Ares allowed Achilles to continue to live. If Ares had not, Zeus would have struck him with a thunderbolt and imprisoned him in Tartarus, the place in the Land of the Dead where evildoers are tormented.

The Greeks stripped the armor from the corpses of their enemies, and Achilles continued to regret killing Penthesilea. He grieved for her much as he had grieved for Patroclus.

Thersites, the ugliest warrior among the Greeks, was also the most despised because of his personality. He delighted in criticizing other people, including Achilles, Agamemnon, Odysseus, and other warriors of much higher rank than he. Thersites looked at Achilles and knew that Achilles regretted killing Penthesilea. Openly mocking Achilles, Thersites said, "Achilles, why are you so concerned about a dead woman, even if she is an Amazon? She wanted to kill many of us Greeks, and yet you care about her death. Are you mad for women? Do you regard Penthesilea the way you would regard a woman whom you court with gifts so that she may become your bride? Your priorities are in the wrong place. Penthesilea should have killed you with one of her javelins. That would be better than being mad for women. Achilles, you are not yourself. Wise up. Think of Paris, who was and is mad for Helen. Think of what has happened to the Trojans as a result of Paris' lust. Lust can make a wise man a fool, and so it is better to seek glory in battle. Be a soldier and kill. The alternative is to be another Paris. Get your joy in battle, not in bed with a woman. Bed is where a coward like Paris gets his joy. You, Achilles, are a coward."

Quick to anger, and not a man to lightly endure an insult, Achilles punched Thersites as hard as he could on the jaw below an ear. With his blood gushing and his teeth falling from his mouth, Thersites fell to the ground and died.

Because Thersites was so disliked, the Greeks were happy that he was dead. One of the Greek warriors said, "Despite being an inferior man, Thersites constantly criticized kings. Such criticism is not right. Themis, the goddess of justice, despises such criticism. Ate, the goddess also known as Ruin, punishes such criticism, as we can see here and now."

Still angry, Achilles said to the corpse of Thersites, "Lie there, dead. You deserve it. You criticized Odysseus, and he hit you hard but did not kill you. I am not as merciful as Odysseus. Go now to the Land of the Dead and insult the ghosts there."

Only one Greek was angry at the death of Thersites: Diomedes, who was related to him. Agrius and Oeneus were brothers. Thersites was the son of Agrius. Diomedes was the son of Tydeus, who was the son of Oeneus. Diomedes was tempted to fight Achilles, but friends spoke to both Diomedes and Achilles and persuaded them not to fight each other.

Priam learned of the death of Penthesilea, and he sent a herald to Agamemnon and Menelaus to ask for the return of her corpse and her armor. Priam wanted to give the Amazon a worthy funeral and to put her ashes in the tomb of Laomedon, his father. Agamemnon and Menelaus were so impressed with Penthesilea's fighting ability that they honored Priam's request and gave her corpse and armor to the Trojans to carry back to Troy.

Priam ordered a funeral pyre built in front of the city, and the Trojans burned Penthesilea's corpse and her armor. After her corpse had been burned to bones, the Trojans put out the fire with wine, and then they collected her bones and put them in a chest. The Trojans grieved as they placed the bones of Penthesilea by the bones of Laomedon. Penthesilea and the twelve Amazons she had brought with her had all died during their first day of battle at Troy.

During a truce with the Greeks, the Trojans also held proper funerals for the other dead Amazons and for the Trojans who had died in the battle. Agamemnon and Menelaus felt no anger toward the dead enemy soldiers.

The Greeks also held funerals for their fallen warriors. Most of the dead warriors were burned together on a common funeral pyre, but Podarces was especially respected and was burned on a separate funeral pyre. Afterwards, they built a mound over his bones. Podarces was the brother of Protesilaus, who was the first Greek to be killed in the Trojan War; he died as the Greek ships landed on the Trojan shore at the beginning of the war.

Thersites' bones were buried separately, away from the bones of the other Greek warriors. His bones were not worthy enough to be buried with the bones of heroes.

After the funerals of the Greeks, Achilles and the other Greek heroes feasted with Agamemnon.

Chapter 2: The Story of Memnon

The next morning, the morale of the Greeks was high, but the morale of many Trojans was low. The Trojans kept watch on their walls; they were afraid that Achilles would conquer the city and burn it.

Thymoetes, an aged advisor, said, "I worry about the future of Troy, now that Hector is no longer alive to protect it. He was our greatest warrior, but Achilles killed him. Achilles is so powerful that he can defeat even gods on the battlefield. Achilles also killed Penthesilea and her Amazons. I had thought that Penthesilea must be a goddess come to us from Mount Olympus to help us resist the Greeks. Obviously, I was wrong. Now we should decide what we ought to do. Should we continue to fight, or should we flee from the city? Now that Achilles is fighting, I do not see how we can be victorious against the Greeks."

Priam replied, "Let us not flee the city. Also, let us not fight the Greeks on the battlefield. Instead, let us stay behind our walls and resist the Greeks. We have powerful allies coming to fight with and for us. Memnon, king of Ethiopia, land of black people, is coming to Troy with an army. I think that by now he must be close to Troy. I sent him a message asking for his help, and he replied that he would help us. We Trojans should stay here and fight. To run away and live among foreigners would be a disgrace."

Polydamas spoke next in the council: "If Memnon is really coming to us to help us, we should wait for him. However, I worry that he and his warriors will die in battle as they fight for us. Now that Achilles is fighting again, the Greek army is much stronger. I do not think that we should flee from Troy, but I also do not think that we should die in battle. I recommend that we give Helen, Menelaus' lawfully wedded wife, back to the Greeks, along with all the treasure that Paris took when he sailed away with Helen and returned to Troy. As war reparations in the tenth year of this war, we can offer twice as much treasure as Paris stole. That would be better than to have our city conquered and set on fire. I believe that this is the best plan. Previously, I urged Hector to be cautious, but he ignored my advice. It would have been much better for him and for us if he had taken my advice."

Many Trojans believed that Polydamas' advice was good, but they did not say so openly because they respected Priam, whom they thought would reject Polydamas' advice. They did not want to upset their king.

Paris, who had run away with Helen, over whom the war was being fought, did not want to give her back to Menelaus. Paris said, "Polydamas, in war you are a weak coward. In council, you believe that you give the best advice, but you are wrong. It is best for you to stay in Troy and not fight, while I lead real warriors into battle. Real men find pleasure in fighting in war; women and children find pleasure in running away from war. You also find pleasure in running away from war."

Not one to say one thing behind a man's back and a different thing to that man's face, Polydamas said to Paris, "Your adultery will destroy your city and your people. I hope that I am never as selfish and as rash as you. I want to keep my home and my family safe. You say that I lack courage, but what kind of courage have you had? You have had the courage to steal the lawfully wedded wife of another man. You have had the courage to plunge your city into war. You have had the courage to get many of your fellow warriors killed. I want no part of that kind of courage."

Paris did not answer. He knew that many Trojans had died so that he and Helen could have an adulterous love affair, and he knew that many more Trojans would die so that he and Helen could continue to have an adulterous love affair. But he preferred sleeping with Helen and watching many Trojans die to giving Helen back to her husband. He himself was willing to risk dying rather than give back Helen.

Soon after the council, Memnon and his army of Ethiopians arrived. Sailors rejoice when they see the stars of the Great Bear after a dangerous storm, and the Trojans rejoiced to see so many new allies. Priam rejoiced. He thought that now the Trojans and their allies could burn the Greek ships because Memnon was a huge warrior and his army contained many battle-ready warriors eager to win glory by killing Greeks. Priam gave Memnon many gifts, and he gave everyone a feast.

Priam and Memnon talked to each other at the feast. Priam spoke about the Greek warriors and the war. Memnon spoke about his parents: the immortal Dawn and the mortal Tithonus. Memnon also told Priam about his journey from Ethiopia to Troy. He and his warriors had fought and defeated an army of

Solymi soldiers in southwest Asia Minor who had attempted to keep him from reaching Troy. Memnon also told Priam about the many other peoples he had encountered.

Priam said to Memnon, "The gods have granted me one of my wishes by allowing me to see you and your warriors who have come to fight for Troy. I hope that the gods continue to grant me wishes. I want to see the Greeks die at the end of your spear and your warriors' spears. You and your warriors resemble gods. Tonight, you and your warriors can feast. Later, you and your warriors can go into battle."

Priam then toasted Memnon with a huge golden cup that Hephaestus had given to Zeus when Hephaestus had married Aphrodite. Zeus had given the cup to Dardanus, the founder of Troy, and the cup had since passed from one king of Troy to another as father passed it on to son: Dardanus to Erichthonius to Tros to Ilus to Laomedon to Priam. Priam had planned to give the huge golden cup to Hector, but fate made that impossible.

Memnon said to Priam, "A feast is a time for enjoying oneself, not for making boasts. Soon enough, you will see for yourself whether I am a brave man or a coward in battle. Right now, however, it is time for my warriors and me to sleep. For us to be ready to fight, we need to sleep and not drink too much wine."

Priam replied, "You are right. Do as you wish. A good host ought not to force a guest to stay at a feast longer than he wishes, and a good host ought not to force a guest to leave a feast sooner than he wishes."

Memnon left the banquet and went to sleep — the last sleep that he would have in the Land of the Living. The other banqueters also left the feast and went to sleep.

The gods were also feasting on Mount Olympus. Zeus gave them orders about the next day's battle: "Tomorrow, many warriors and many horses will die in the battle. I order all of you not to interfere in the battle. Some of you will regret the deaths of some of the mortals. I order each of you not to request that I prolong any mortal's life past the time that he is fated to die."

The gods would obey the orders of Zeus: He was powerful, and they were afraid of him. Even if a god's or a goddess' son were to die in battle the next day, that god or goddess would not go against the will of Zeus.

The next morning, Memnon woke up early. He was eager to go to war. On this day, the Trojans and their allies would fight on the battlefield in front of Troy. As the armed Trojans and Ethiopians and other Trojan allies poured onto the battleground, they looked like black storm clouds or like great clouds of locusts that devour grain and bring famine to humans.

Achilles and the other Greeks put on their armor. Achilles' armor shone like lightning. It shone like the Sun that brings light to humans. The Greek soldiers followed Achilles, and the Trojans and their allies followed Memnon.

The battle started, and the Ethiopians fought well as the two opposing armies crashed against each other like huge waves in a sea disturbed by winds coming from changing directions. The two armies crashed against each other, making a sound like that of a swollen river as it pours into the sea as rain pelts the ground and thunder booms and lightning strikes.

Achilles killed the Trojans Thalius and Mentes and many other warriors with his spear. Achilles was like an earthquake that assaults buildings.

Memnon killed many Greeks, including Pheron with a spear to the chest. Memnon also killed Ereuthus. Pheron and Ereuthus, whose king was Nestor, had been eager to fight in battle. Memnon then tried to kill Nestor, but Antilochus, Nestor's son, stood in front of his father to defend him. Antilochus threw his spear at Memnon, but Memnon swerved aside and Antilochus' spear narrowly missed him and instead killed the Ethiopian named Aethops.

Angry at the death of Aethops, Memnon rushed at Antilochus, who threw a rock at him and hit him. Memnon's sturdy helmet saved his life. Now angrier, Memnon was like a lion rushing at a boar that is dangerous and knows how to defend itself. Memnon speared Antilochus in the heart. Antilochus, the son of Nestor and the friend of Achilles, was dead.

Having seen his son die in front of him, Nestor grieved. Antilochus had given his life in order to save the life of his father. No grief is worse than the grief a father feels when a son dies.

Nestor called to Thrasymedes, another of his sons, "Come here and help me to kill Memnon, who has killed Antilochus. If we cannot kill Memnon, then let us die fighting him. This is not the time to fear Memnon; we should be like my brother Periclymenus, who was not afraid to fight Heracles, although Heracles killed him and all of my other brothers. Sometimes, a weaker man must fight a stronger man."

Thrasymedes came quickly, as did the Greek Phereus. They were eager to fight Memnon. They were like two hunters running toward a boar or a bear that is eager to fight them.

Thrasymedes and Phereus threw their spears. They missed Memnon but killed Trojan warriors. Phereus' spear killed Polymnius, the son of Meges. Thrasymedes, angry at the death of his brother Antilochus, killed Laomedon.

Memnon busied himself stripping the armor off Antilochus' corpse. Memnon knew that as a warrior he was much the superior of Thrasymedes and Phereus, and he did not fear them. Having thrown their spears, Thrasymedes and Phereus were like two jackals that were afraid to attack a lion that was standing over a stag.

Nestor ordered other warriors to attack Memnon. He also wanted to personally attack the warrior who had killed his son. Nestor would have died at the end of the spear of Memnon, but Memnon saw that Nestor was an elderly man — as old as Memnon's father — and said to him, "Aged sir, I ought not to fight you — you are so much older than I am. Before, when I charged you, I thought that you were a much younger warrior and a worthy opponent for me to kill. Please back away from the fighting, or I may be forced to kill you although I am much younger and much stronger than you. Don't be a fool: You ought not to attack a warrior so much younger and stronger than you."

Nestor replied, "No one will call me a fool: It is not foolish to try to kill a man who has killed one's son and to try to recover the corpse of the son in order to give it a proper funeral. But instead you stand there boasting — you are so young, and your mind is so proud. I wish I were younger and had the strength of my youth. If that were the case, you would be dead. But I am burdened by the indignities of old age. I am like an aged lion that a dog has chased away from a sheepfold. The lion cannot kill the dog because the lion has lost its teeth and its strength. But despite being as old as I am, I am still better than many younger men."

Nestor backed away from Memnon and from the corpse of Antilochus. Thrasymedes and Phereus also backed away: Memnon was a mighty warrior — mightier than they were. A river can rush toward the sea, swollen by the rain of a storm, with Zeus' thunderbolts crashing down. So Memnon rushed across the battlefield, killing Greeks and forcing them to the sea. His Ethiopian warriors also killed many Greek warriors, spilling their blood onto the ground. Many

Greek corpses lay on the ground, but Memnon kept on killing. He wanted to be a hero to the Trojans and a terror to the Greeks, but his fate was coming closer to him.

Many strong and confident Ethiopian warriors fought beside Memnon: Alcyoneus, Alexippus, Asiades, Clydon, Meneclus, Nychius, and others.

Nestor killed Meneclus, and in retaliation Memnon killed several Greek warriors. He was like a hunter who with other hunters has driven a herd of deer into a trap of nets and throws javelins and kills swift does as the hunting dogs bark. Memnon's Ethiopians rejoiced at the slaughter Memnon was creating, and the Greek warriors fled from him.

Zeus sometimes hurls a thunderbolt and breaks off a crag from a mountain. The crag rolls down the mountain, and sheep in its path try to flee and avoid destruction. Just like those frightened sheep, the Greek warriors tried to flee from Memnon.

Nestor found Achilles and said to him, "My son Antilochus, your friend, is dead. Memnon has killed him and stripped his armor. If Memnon keeps the corpse, he will feed it to dogs and birds. Please help recover the corpse — Antilochus was your friend!"

Achilles had been killing many Trojans on a part of the battlefield away from Memnon, but now — angry at the death of his friend Antilochus — he ran toward Memnon, who lifted a huge rock that marked the boundary of a wheat field and threw it at Achilles and hit his shield — which protected him.

Fighting on foot, Achilles injured Memnon — Achilles' spear struck Memnon's right shoulder. But Memnon's spear also drew blood as it grazed Achilles' arm.

Memnon said to Achilles, "I think that this is your day to die. You have killed many Trojans, and you have boasted both that you are the greatest warrior at Troy and that your mother is a goddess: an immortal Nereid, a sea-goddess whose father is the sea-god Nereus.

"But I also have divine parentage. My mother is the immortal goddess Dawn, who brings light to the world, and the immortal nymphs known as the Hesperides raised me. One of the reasons that I am not afraid of you is that my divine mother is superior to your divine mother. My mother provides light for immortal gods and mortal humans that allows them to work to accomplish many good things. Your mother hides in the sea with the fish. Few see her, and she accomplishes nothing of value. I do not respect your mother — she is only a minor sea-goddess."

Achilles replied, "Why have you come to Troy to challenge me? I am stronger and more skilled in war than you. My lineage is better than yours. Zeus is one of my ancestors. My father is Peleus, whose father is Aeacus, whose father is Zeus, and so my great-grandfather is Zeus.

"The sea-nymphs known as the Nereids are the daughters of Nereus, and they are honored by the Olympian gods. The Nereid who is most honored by the Olympian gods is my mother, Thetis, because of her wisdom that she uses to help the gods. She helped the god Dionysus when Lycurgus, the king of Thrace, persecuted him and imprisoned his followers, who are known as the Maenads. Dionysus fled and Thetis hid him until he could get revenge on Lycurgus. Thetis also helped Hephaestus the blacksmith god, Hephaestus was born with lame legs, and his mother, Hera, threw him from Mount Olympus because of his lame legs. The immortals Thetis and Eurynome took care of him for nine years. Hephaestus showed his skill as a blacksmith and an artist early; he made beautiful jewelry. Thetis also aided Zeus when three gods — Hera, his wife; Poseidon, his brother who is the god of the sea; and Athena, his daughter — had succeeded in chaining him. Thetis stayed loyal to Zeus. She, alone of all the many gods, rushed to Zeus and broke the chains that bound him. In addition, she ordered the giant with a hundred hands to go to Zeus and protect him. The gods call the giant Briareus, and the mortals call him Aegaeon. Hera, Poseidon, and Athena saw the giant with the hundred hands. Terrified, they stopped rebelling against Zeus and instead respected him. For all of these reasons, the Olympians honor and respect Thetis.

"You will regret insulting my mother when my spear is in your body. When my friend Patroclus died, I was angry and I killed Hector. Now that my friend Antilochus has died, I am angry and I will kill you. I am not a weak warrior. But let us stop talking. Now is the time to fight!"

Achilles and Memnon fought with swords. The two warriors were nearly equal in fighting strength and ability, and both wore divine armor made by Hephaestus. The two warriors fought so hard and so close that the plumes on their helmets touched. Zeus respected both warriors, and he gave both warriors strength. Eris, the goddess of discord, also respected both warriors. Swords clanged against shields, breastplates, and greaves.

The Trojans and the Ethiopians continued to fight the Greeks, and the dust created by their fighting filled the air. Fog can rise on a mountain in rainy weather when water fills the streams and creeks; shepherds fear for their flocks because wolves take advantage of fog and make raids on the shepherds' livelihood. The dust rising on the battlefield was like the fog rising on a mountain; dust and fog both hide the Sun.

One of the gods dissipated the dust, but no god stopped the fighting. The Fates dealt out death to warriors, and Ares was happy to see so much blood. The plain between the Simois and the Xanthus rivers became a temporary resting place for corpses.

Achilles and Memnon continued to fight each other, and the gods watched. The immortal relatives of Achilles and Memnon feared for them. Thetis and her sisters, the Nereids, were afraid that Achilles might die. Dawn and her nieces, the daughters of Helios, her brother, were afraid that Memnon might die.

These immortal relatives were tempted to join the fight, but Zeus ordered two Fates to go to Achilles and Memnon. The dark Fate went to Memnon; the bright Fate went to Achilles. A shout went out from the immortals as the Fates took their positions. The immortals supporting Memnon grieved; the immortals supporting Achilles rejoiced.

Achilles and Memnon were fighting so hard that they did not notice the Fates. Each warrior concentrated on his enemy: a worthy opponent. It seemed as if a giant were fighting a Titan. Each warrior tried to kill the other by wielding a sword or throwing a huge rock. Sometimes, a weapon hit a warrior, but the warrior continued to fight. Neither warrior showed fear. Each warrior was like a headland jutting out into water. Storms assault the headland, but the headland resists the winds and waves.

Achilles and Memnon both had divine ancestry, including Zeus. Memnon's father was Tithonus, a son of King Laomedon of Troy. One of Laomedon's ancestors was Dardanus, the son of Zeus. Because Achilles and Memnon were both related to Zeus, Enyo, goddess of war, made them almost evenly matched as they fought each other.

The two opposing armies were also almost evenly matched. Each warrior received at least one wound, and blood and sweat dripped from each warrior onto the ground. Corpses covered the ground as clouds sometimes cover the sky and make sailors afraid. The corpses were as numerous as the fallen leaves at the beginning of winter, and horses trampled the corpses.

Achilles and Memnon continued to fight, and Eris lifted up her scales. Previously, the fate of Achilles in one scale and the fate of Memnon in the other scale had been equal, but now Achilles' fate rose and Memnon's fate fell. Achilles thrust his sword through Memnon's chest, and Memnon fell, terrifying his Ethiopian warriors and his Trojan allies. The Myrmidons, Achilles' warriors, stripped off Memnon's armor, and the Trojans fled. Achilles ran after them.

Memnon's mother, Dawn, grieved, and she covered herself with clouds. She requested that the winds go to the corpse of her son and lift it and carry it away. Drops of blood fell from the corpse, and the gods gathered them and put them in one place and used them to create the Paphlagonian River under Mount Ida. On the anniversary of the day that Memnon died, the river turns red and stinks like a festering wound.

A god gave the Ethiopians a special power. Veiled in fog, they flew behind the corpse of Memnon as the winds carried it away just like the friends of a hunter who has been killed by a boar or a lion carry his corpse away so that it can receive a proper funeral. The hunter's friends mourned, and the Ethiopians mourned.

The Trojans and the Greeks were amazed at the disappearance of the Ethiopians, who went with the corpse of Memnon to a bank of the Aesepus River where is now a grove sacred to the water-nymphs who are the daughters of the river-god Aesepus. The water-nymphs mourned the death of Memnon and planted the trees of the grove around his tomb.

Night arrived, and Dawn came down from the sky. The twelve maidens who are the Zodiac came with her to mourn the death of her son. These twelve maidens are the daughters of the Sun. The seven females who are the Pleiades also came to mourn.

Dawn hugged the body of her son and said, "You are dead, and I mourn the loss of your life. I no longer want to bring light to the sky above the earth. Instead, I want to go to the Land of the Dead and be with you and bring light there. In the Land of the Living and on Mount Olympus, let there be darkness and chaos. Why shouldn't Zeus grieve, too? I am a goddess. I do not deserve this grief. I bring light, a great good to all — but Zeus did not care about my light, or he would not have let you die. So I prefer to go to the Land of the

Dead to be with you. If Zeus wants light, then let him get Thetis, the mother of the warrior who killed you, to provide that light. Now that you are dead, I prefer darkness to light. I do not want Achilles to be able to see with the light I provide."

Dawn cried as she spoke, and the ground by the corpse grew wet. Night also mourned the death of Dawn's son, and clouds hid the stars. Inside Troy, Priam and the other Trojans mourned the death of Memnon. Even the Greeks were not entirely happy. They honored Achilles, but they wept for Antilochus.

Dawn mourned all night, and she did not think about returning to the sky in the morning. She hated Mount Olympus. Beside her, her horses grew uneasy and stomped on the unfamiliar soil; they were eager to pull Dawn's chariot and bring light to the world. Zeus, knowing that Dawn was mourning, sent thunder and lightning and made the earth tremble. He was warning Dawn that he would be angry if light did not shine on the earth. Zeus is dangerous, and he is powerful, and Dawn, despite her grief, was afraid.

The Ethiopians buried Memnon, and then Dawn changed them into birds that are called Memnons. They still fly around his tomb and drop earth on it. To honor their fallen king, they hold games for him. They divide into two groups and play at war, with one group attacking the other group. Sometimes, one group of birds wins. Sometimes, each group of birds "kills" the opposing group. These games held to honor her son please Dawn. They also please Memnon, wherever he is: in the darkness of Hades or in the light of the Elysian Fields.

The goddesses known as the Horae persuaded Dawn, unwilling as she was, to return to the sky and bring light to the world. Despite her grief, she obeyed them because she was afraid of the might of Zeus. The Pleiades returned to the sky before Dawn did, but Dawn herself opened the gates and drove her chariot into the sky to banish the darkness and bring her light into the world.

Chapter 3: The Death of Achilles

When dawn arrived, the Greeks, mourning, buried the body of Antilochus. The Greeks honored Nestor, who endured his grief without collapsing. Nestor was a strong man.

Angry because of the death of his friend, Achilles armed himself. The Trojans, despite the deaths of their allies Penthesilea and Memnon, came from behind their walls and prepared to battle the Greeks. On this day, many warriors would die, including Achilles.

Achilles killed many Trojan warriors. The ground that gives us life grew red with blood, and the waters of the Simois and Xanthus rivers could not reach the sea because Trojan corpses dammed them. Achilles killed Trojans right up to the gates of Troy. He could have smashed open the gates and conquered the city that day, but Apollo himself opposed him. Apollo flew from Mount Olympus to Troy, stood in front of Achilles, and warned him, "Back away from Troy — now! You have killed enough Trojans. If you do not back away from Troy, one of the gods may kill you."

Achilles did not fear Apollo or his words. Achilles replied, "I prefer not to battle against a god, although I will if I have to. You have tricked me before. You once surrounded Hector with fog and kept him away from my spear. Later, I was killing Trojans and chasing them back to Troy. You assumed the form of a Trojan, and I chased you, hoping to kill you, and you led me away from the city. Through your trick, you delayed the death of Hector and saved the lives of many Trojans. Apollo, *you* need to leave Troy and go back to Mount Olympus, or I may end up fighting you — even if you are an immortal god."

Achilles turned away from Apollo and continued to chase and kill Trojans.

Apollo thought, *Achilles is insane to resist my will and my orders. He has made a big mistake. Zeus and the other gods are not going to protect him.*

At the Scaean Gates of Troy, Apollo wrapped mist around himself and fitted an arrow to his bow. He shot the arrow and hit Achilles on the ankle. Achilles fell like a tower that an earthquake has knocked over.

Achilles shouted, "Who has hit me with an arrow? Reveal yourself so that I can kill you! My spear will shed your blood and pull out your intestines and send your ghost to the Land of the Dead! No one — no matter how much courage he has — can withstand my spear. You were able to wound me only because you were hidden from me. Even if you are a god, even if you are Apollo, reveal yourself. My mother, Thetis, told me that Apollo would kill me at the Scaean Gates of Troy. The arrows of the immortals kill."

Achilles pulled out the arrow and threw it away, but the winds carried it back to Apollo, who caught it as he returned to Mount Olympus. The arrows of the immortal gods are also immortal.

On Mount Olympus, the gods were accustomed to watch the Trojan War as a form of entertainment.

Hera, who supported the Greeks, said to Apollo, who supported the Trojans, "Why have you shot Achilles with an arrow that will kill him? Have you forgotten the marriage of his parents? The mortal Peleus married the immortal Thetis. You played your lyre and sang at the wedding to celebrate their union. Your audience — gods, people, beasts, and birds — listened eagerly to your songs. You even prayed that Peleus and Thetis would have a son. You have forgotten all of this and have killed Achilles.

"And why did you kill Achilles? To please the Trojans, although you worked a year for Laomedon, king of Troy. You tended his flocks, and he cheated you out of your pay and forced you and Poseidon, who had also worked a year for Laomedon, to leave Troy. You and Poseidon had offended Zeus, and he forced you to work for Laomedon.

"So now you have killed Achilles, yet his ancestry included immortals and he respected the gods. Can't you tell which mortals deserve to die, and which mortals deserve to live?

"Even though you have killed Achilles, the war will not become easier for the Trojans because Achilles' son, Neoptolemus, will come immediately to the war to replace him. Neoptolemus is strong like his father, and he will kill many Trojans. Now that you have killed Achilles, how will you be able to look his mother, Thetis, in the eyes? She has always respected you."

Apollo did not reply to Hera. He sat and looked at the floor. The gods who supported the Greeks were angry at him, but the gods who supported the Trojans were happy. They praised Apollo, but they praised him when Hera was not present — they did not want to make Hera angry.

Achilles was still fighting; his blood still ran hot in his body. Because Achilles was dangerous although he was wounded, many of the Trojans stayed a distance away from him, the way they would stay a distance away from a lion that a hunter has mortally wounded. Despite its wound, which will kill it, the lion still roars and its jaws and talons are still deadly.

Achilles speared Orythaon, one of Hector's friends, in the temple, cutting through his helmet and skull and destroying his brain. Achilles then killed Hipponous with a spear in the face — one of Hipponous' eyes fell onto the ground. Achilles then killed Alcathous with a spear to the jaw — the spear cut off Alcathous' tongue and came out through his ear. These three Trojans had rushed at Achilles, trying to kill him. Achilles also killed many other Trojans who tried to run away from him.

But Achilles' blood grew cold and he lost his strength. He could no longer run. He stood and leaned on his spear, and he shouted at the Trojans who were running away from him, "You are cowards. Even after I am dead, you will still die — I will send Furies after you to kill you! That will be my revenge for the way I died!"

The Trojans heard Achilles' shout, and they were terrified the way a fawn is terrified when it hears the roar of a lion. Achilles' shout was so strong that many Trojans did not think he was wounded. But Achilles, as strong as he was, was unable to resist the wound caused by Apollo. He fell to the ground and added his corpse to the many other corpses lying there. Even though Achilles was dead, the Trojans stared at his corpse from a distance — they were so afraid of Achilles that they did not want to come close to his corpse. Sheep are terrified of lions, and even after a shepherd has killed a lion, the sheep are too afraid to come close to the lion's corpse.

Paris rejoiced at the death of Achilles because he hoped that the Greeks would leave Troy and sail home, and he encouraged his Trojans to seize Achilles' corpse: "Let us fight to get his body. Today, either the Greeks will kill us or we will drag Achilles' corpse to Troy behind Hector's horses. Because Hector is dead, I am using his horses, although they are still mourning the death of their master. If we can take Achilles' corpse to Troy, we will win honor for Hector and for his horses. If the ghosts in Hades have intelligence and feeling, Hector's ghost will rejoice that we have the corpse of the warrior who has killed so many Trojans and Trojan allies.

"If we take the corpse of Achilles back to Troy, we will make happy the Trojan women who have lost a husband, a father, a brother, or a son because of

Achilles. The Trojan women will gather around the corpse of Achilles the way that lionesses gather around a hunter who has attacked their cubs. My father, Priam, will be happy. The old men of Troy will also be happy when they see the corpse of Achilles provide food for birds."

The Trojans and Trojan allies who had previously been afraid of Achilles now surrounded his corpse. Glaucus, Aeneas, Agenor, and other warriors were eager for Hector's horses to drag the corpse to Troy.

But Great Ajax stood over Achilles' corpse and defended it with his spear as the Trojans attacked him. The Trojans were like bees attacking a man who is harvesting their honey. The smoke brought by the harvester of honey bothers the bees, and the harvester of honey attends to his work. Great Ajax' spear hurt the Trojans as Great Ajax kept possession of Achilles' corpse.

Great Ajax killed Agelaus, Ocythous, Agestratus, Aganippus, Zorus, Nissus, and Erymas. Erymas fought for Glaucus, the leader of the Trojans' allies from Lycia. Glaucus mourned Erymas' death and attacked Great Ajax and stabbed his shield, which protected him. The shield was made of eight layers: seven oxhides and a top layer of bronze.

Glaucus said to Great Ajax, "The Greeks consider you to be their best warrior: the equal of Achilles. But Achilles is dead, and I think that today you will die."

Great Ajax replied, "You are a fool. Hector was a much better warrior than you, and he stayed away from me in battle. He was intelligent. But you seek to battle me although you are much weaker than I am. You will not be able to escape death at my hands the way you escaped death at the hands of Diomedes. You and I are not hereditary friends, the way that you and Diomedes are. Because your ancestors had been friends, you and Diomedes were hereditary friends, and you and he exchanged armor and did not fight each other. The armor you gave Diomedes was worth one hundred oxen, and the bronze armor that you received from Diomedes was worth only nine oxen. That was a good deal for both of you. Diomedes became richer, and you saved your life. But I am willing to kill you and anyone who fights alongside you. I am willing to send you and others to the Land of the Dead."

Great Ajax then attacked the Trojans and their Lycian allies and killed many warriors. The Trojans were afraid of Great Ajax the way that fish are afraid of a hungry dolphin. Nevertheless, they continued to fight him. Corpses lay on the ground around Great Ajax just like the corpses of boars lay on the ground around a lion.

Great Ajax speared and killed Glaucus, who fell onto the corpse of Achilles just like a small tree can fall at the foot of a huge tree. Aeneas fought Great Ajax and recovered Glaucus' corpse, which the Lycians carried back to Troy as they mourned the death of their leader.

Aeneas continued to fight Great Ajax, who speared him above the bicep of Aeneas' right arm. Aeneas retreated from Great Ajax and returned to Troy, where healers took care of him.

Great Ajax kept fighting, and his spear was like bolts of lightning that flash and kill. As he fought, he mourned the death of Achilles.

Fighting now alongside Great Ajax was Odysseus, the son of Laertes of the island of Ithaca. Odysseus killed Maenalus, Oresbius, Atymnius, and other warriors. Atymnius' mother was the nymph Pegasis. Oresbius' mother was Panacea, the goddess of universal remedy, who could heal all diseases but who could not welcome her son home alive from the war.

Alcon wounded Odysseus with a spear near his right knee. His blood gushed out, but Odysseus speared Alcon. The spear went through Alcon's shield and pierced his flesh, and Alcon fell onto the ground. Odysseus pulled his spear out of Alcon's body, and as the spear exited Alcon's body, so did his breath. Alcon breathed no more.

Despite his wound, Odysseus stayed and fought.

Other Greeks also fought around the corpse of Achilles and speared many Trojans. When autumn arrives, many leaves fall to the ground. The Greeks used their spears to make many Trojans fall to the ground. The Greeks — especially Great Ajax — wanted to take the corpse of Achilles back to their ships so they could give it a proper burial.

Paris aimed an arrow at Great Ajax, but Great Ajax saw Paris and threw a rock at him and shattered his helmet. Paris fell, unconscious, and his arrows littered the ground. Paris' friends grabbed him and used Hector's horses to carry him to Troy. They also picked up his arrows and carried them to Troy. Paris recovered consciousness and groaned.

Great Ajax shouted at Paris, "You have escaped death today, but soon you will die. I may kill you, or some other Greek will kill you. Right now, I am more concerned with taking the corpse of my friend back to our ships."

Great Ajax kept fighting, and he scattered the Trojans, who were afraid. Great Ajax was like a mighty eagle that scatters worthless vultures that are eating the remains of sheep killed by wolves. The Trojans were afraid of Great Ajax the way that starlings are afraid of a hawk that pursues and kills them. Great Ajax, covered with the blood of Trojans and Trojan allies, chased the Trojans as they fled to Troy. The Trojans fled through the open gates and closed them. Great Ajax had penned the Trojans the way that a shepherd pens sheep.

Great Ajax walked back to the corpse of Achilles, but his feet not once touched the ground. Instead, he stepped on bloody armor and bloody bodies. Farmers reap grain and place sheaves on the ground. Fate had reaped lives and placed many corpses on the ground. The corpses no longer thought about war.

The Greeks did not strip the armor off their fallen enemies. Instead, they attended to the funeral of Achilles. They carried his corpse to their camps and ships, and they mourned his death — the death of their mightiest warrior.

In ancient times, Tityos tried to rape Leto, the mother of Apollo, who defended her and killed Tityos with many arrows. Tityos was so huge that his corpse covered many acres of his mother, the earth, who mourned his death. Leto, however, laughed at the death of Tityos. The Greeks mourned the death of Achilles, but the Trojans laughed.

The Greeks mourned the death of Achilles, and they wondered if the Trojans would defeat and kill them in battle. They also remembered their parents, their wives, and their children at home, and this also caused them to mourn. They lay on the sand around Achilles' body, and they pulled out their hair and poured sand on their heads. When a city is conquered, its citizens grieve as the city burns and the enemy warriors kill the city's defenders. Like that, the Greeks grieved for Achilles, whom a divinely made arrow shot by a god had killed. No mortal and no mortal weapon had killed Achilles. Athena once threw a rock at Ares in battle, and Ares fell. Achilles looked just like the fallen Ares.

Achilles' warriors, the Myrmidons, mourned his death. To them, Achilles had been a friend. He had not been arrogant to them; he had been gentle and intelligent and not just mighty in battle.

Great Ajax and Achilles were related, as both had Zeus as an ancestor, and Great Ajax mourned Achilles both as a friend and as a relative. Great Ajax said, "Achilles, you died at Troy, far from your home. An arrow — the weapon of a coward — killed you. Real warriors fight up close, spear-to-spear or sword-to-sword. Those who are capable of fighting up close do so. They hold a shield, and they use their spears or swords to pierce the enemy's chest. They do not shoot arrows from a safe distance. If the archer who had shot you had instead run at you with a spear, he would be dead and you would be alive.

"Your death must be the result of the will of Zeus, who must be planning victory for the Trojans. We have worked hard to defeat Troy, but now Zeus is against us.

"Soon, Achilles, your aged father, Peleus, will learn about your death. He may die when he learns that you are dead. That may be best because it will end his grief. If he lives, he will have to further endure a grim old age without his son to comfort and protect him. The gods gave him a son to be proud of, but the gods did not give him a son who will comfort him in his extreme old age. A son ought not to die before his father dies."

Phoenix, the old man who had helped raise Achilles, and who had served as an advisor to him, said, "I wish that I had died before you died. I have never felt this kind of grief before, not even when I left my parents and went into exile. Your father, Peleus, let me live in his palace. When you, Achilles, were a small child, your father let me look after you as if you were my own son. You spoke baby talk, and you spit up on my shirt. I laughed as I took care of you because I believed that when I grew old, you would take care of me. You grew up to be a brave warrior, as your father and I wanted, but now you are in the eternal darkness. I want to die now, before your father learns that you are dead. He will grieve as I grieve. He and I will both wish to die soon — that will be better than to continue to live without you."

Agamemnon, the leader of the Greek forces against the Trojans, said, "You are dead, Achilles, although you were our very best warrior. Now that you are dead, the Trojans may very well win this war. Now that you are dead, the Trojans rejoice. When you were still alive, they feared you the way a lamb fears a lion. Instead of hiding behind the high walls of their city, the Trojans will fight on the battlefield in front of our camps. Zeus must have lied to me. He promised that I would conquer Troy, but now that seems to be impossible."

The Greeks all mourned along with their leaders. Their cries rose to the sky. Winds can cause huge waves that crash on the shore. The Greeks' cries rose into the air the way that huge waves rise on the sea.

Nestor, the father of Antilochus, said, "Let us stop mourning long enough to care for Achilles' corpse. We need to wash him, dress him in fine clothing, and lay him on a bier. This is the way to show respect to the dead. We can continue to mourn him for several days after this deed is done."

Agamemnon ordered water to be heated. They washed Achilles' corpse and dressed it in purple clothing that his mother, Thetis, had given to him.

Athena came down from Mount Olympus and sprinkled ambrosia, the food of the gods, over Achilles' head to preserve the corpse and keep it from corruption. She gave Achilles a fierce frown that matched his frown when Patroclus had died. Achilles looked not as if he were dead — he looked as if he were sleeping.

Achilles' slave-women mourned his death. He had won these women and made them slaves when he conquered the island of Lesbos and the city of Thebe. Achilles had killed these women's husbands and brothers and made the women slaves, yet they mourned for him. Although they were slaves, he had treated them well, and now in mourning they beat their breasts and scratched their faces.

Briseis, Achilles' concubine, especially cried aloud. She had scratched bloody welts on her skin; the welts looked like blood dripped on milk. A beautiful woman, she said, "I have suffered much in my life. My husband and my brothers died defending my city and me. But my city fell, and I became a slave. Your death will cause much more suffering for me. You did not force me to do the harsh tasks of most slaves but instead made me your concubine and gave me a better life than most slaves. I hoped to become your wife — being a wife is better than being a slave. But now that you are dead, I will be passed on to another Greek master who will take me away in his ship and force me to live a life of wretchedness and degradation. I wish that I could have died before you died."

The tears fell from Briseis' eyes to the ground the way that frost and ice melt and fall to the ground from the side of a cliff.

The sea-nymphs heard the cries of mourning and realized that Achilles, the son of Thetis, had died. Thetis and her sisters of the sea dressed themselves in dark robes and swam to the shore; the water of the sea made a swift path for them. The Muses also heard the cries of mourning and came to the Greek ships to support Thetis. The Greeks normally would have been afraid to see even one immortal so close, but Zeus gave them courage, and many mortals and many immortals mourned together.

Thetis kissed the lips of her dead son and said, "The goddess Dawn will be happy that you are dead because you killed Memnon, her son. The god of the river Axius will be happy that you are dead because you killed Asteropaeus, his grandson. The Trojans will be happy that you are dead because you killed so many Trojans.

"But I will go to Zeus and show him my grief. I did not want to wed a mortal man; Zeus forced me. That mortal man, Peleus, is now very old, and soon the Fates will come for him and he will die. But I mourn for my son rather than for my husband. I resisted going to the marriage bed. I can change shapes, and I turned myself into wind and water and fire so that I would not have to sleep with Peleus. But Zeus had heard that I would give birth to a son who would be greater than his father, and so he married me to a mortal so that the mortal's son would not be so powerful that he could overthrow Zeus. For Zeus' plan to work, I had to give birth to a mortal son. Zeus convinced me to allow myself to be mastered by that mortal man on our marriage bed. Zeus convinced me by telling me how great my son — Achilles — would be. Zeus kept his promise that my son would be glorious and warlike, but Achilles was also short-lived, and so I am in great pain. I will go to Zeus and let him know that I am suffering. Zeus caused my suffering. If I had married a god, then my son would have been immortal."

Calliope, the Muse of epic poetry, said to Thetis, "Other gods have felt the grief that you are feeling. Zeus himself lost many sons in the Trojan War, including Sarpedon. My son Orpheus died because he was mortal, although his skill at playing the lyre and singing made even the trees in a forest listen. I endured, and you must endure. We must accept what the Fates have decreed; they make no exceptions for mortals, not even mortals with a god as a parent. Know that your son will be remembered by future generations. The other Muses and I will inspire poets to remember your son in song. Know also that Troy, the city your son was attempting to conquer, will fall. That, also, is fated."

Night arrived, and many Greeks slept. Thetis, however, could not sleep because of her grief, and the Muses stayed awake with her and tried to comfort her. Thetis' sisters, the sea-nymphs, stayed up and mourned. Thetis' father and other minor sea-gods also mourned.

Dawn, the mother of Memnon, arrived, and she cast a brilliant light on the city of Troy. The Greeks mourned Achilles for days, and then they burned his body with wood taken from Mount Ida. The Greeks put much armor on the funeral pyre — the armor of warriors whom Achilles had killed. They also slaughtered Trojan men and threw them on the pyre along with slaughtered horses and bulls and sheep and fat. Achilles' slave-women threw clothing on the pyre along with gold and amber. The Myrmidons and Briseis cut off locks of their hair and threw them on the pyre. They also put jars of oil and honey and wine and other good things on the pyre.

When the fire had been lit, Zeus sprinkled drops of ambrosia on Achilles, and he sent Hermes the messenger god to Aeolus, the god of the winds, to command him to release the winds so that the funeral pyre would burn with fierce flames. The winds blew all day and all night, and the fire consumed everything. The winds then went back to Aeolus.

The Myrmidons put out the remaining fire with wine, and then they collected the bones of Achilles, which were apart from the other bones. Achilles' bones looked like the bones of a giant. They put his bones in a tomb and built over it a funeral mound. The sea-nymphs had honored Thetis by pouring ambrosia, the drink of the gods, over Achilles' bones before they were buried. Thetis provided a vase to hold the gold and silver casket that held the bones. Hephaestus had made the vase and given it to the god Dionysius, who gave it to Thetis.

Achilles' horses also mourned for him. His horses wanted to leave mortals behind and go back to the land where they had been born, where Zephyrus, the god of the West wind, had mated with Podarge, a Harpy who was the horses' mother. But Achilles' horses did not leave because they were awaiting the arrival of their new master: Neoptolemus, Achilles' son. Achilles' horses knew their fate: First, they would serve Poseidon, then Peleus, then Achilles, and finally Neoptolemus, who would come to Troy from the island of Scyros, and whom they would eventually carry to the Elysian Fields, where blessed souls live happily and well. The horses mourned for Achilles, but they were also eager to see Neoptolemus.

Poseidon came out of the sea and comforted Thetis, "I have good news for you, Thetis. Achilles, your son, will not go down to the Land of the Dead. He will be a god. At one time, Dionysus and Heracles were mortals, but they became gods. So it is with Achilles. I am giving him an island in the Black Sea. He will be a god there, and the people who live in the region will worship him and give him sacrifices. You need not cry any longer."

Poseidon left and returned to the sea, and Thetis felt her grief leave her. Poseidon kept his promise. The Greeks returned to their camps, the Muses returned to Mount Helicon, and the sea-nymphs returned to the sea.

Chapter 4: The Funeral Games to Honor Achilles

While the Greeks mourned the death of Achilles, the Trojans mourned the death of Glaucus. They put Glaucus' body on a funeral pyre outside the Trojan Gates, but Apollo took the body and gave it to the winds to carry to Glaucus' homeland: Lycia. The Lycians buried the body under an unbreakable rock, and nymphs caused water to flow there. People today call that stream the Glaucus.

The Greeks continued to mourn the death of Achilles, a death that made the Trojans happy. Some Trojans said among themselves, "Zeus has given us a generous gift: the death of our most powerful enemy. Now we can have a break — a breathing space — in the war. Achilles killed many of us Trojans, but now I think that the Greeks will sail for their homes. I wish that Hector were still alive — he would kill all the remaining Greeks."

Other Trojans were older and wiser. They said, "The Greeks will not set sail for their homes. Although Achilles is dead, the Greeks will still be eager for battle. The Greeks still have many powerful warriors: Diomedes, Great Ajax, Agamemnon, and Menelaus. Achilles may be dead, but the Greeks still have many warriors whom we ought to fear. If Apollo kills these other powerful Greek warriors, then perhaps the war will end."

The gods had taken sides in the Trojan War. Those gods who supported the Greeks were miserable because Achilles was dead. Those gods who supported the Trojans were happy because Achilles was dead.

Hera, who supported the Greeks, said to Zeus, "Why are you helping the Trojans? You must have forgotten the immortal goddess Thetis, whom you gave in marriage in Peleus, a mortal man. You arranged the marriage, which we immortals attended. We immortals gave Thetis and Peleus many gifts. So why are you helping the Trojans?"

Zeus did not reply. He was planning the end of the war and its aftermath. The Greeks would conquer Troy, but Zeus was planning to give many hardships to the Greeks both during the war and after it ended.

Darkness arrived, and the Greeks ate. Eating is a necessity even for those who grieve. Many Greeks then slept. When Dawn came to light the earth, the Greeks arose. They were still planning to conquer Troy despite their grief because of the death of Achilles. The many Greeks arose and moved like waves whipped by wind or like grains at the ends of wheat stalks whipped by wind.

Diomedes said to the Greek warriors, "Let us go to battle now. The Trojans probably think that we will leave because Achilles has died. Let us show them that they are wrong. Let us win glory in battle."

Great Ajax said, "What you say is good: We will continue to fight the Trojans, and we will continue to win glory in battle. However, first we need to wait for Thetis, who will come from the sea to hold funeral games for her son. She spoke to me yesterday, apart from other Greeks, and she told me what she was planning. She will arrive quickly. Also, the Trojans are likely to stay behind their walls and not leave the city and fight. Achilles is dead, but of course you and Agamemnon and I are still alive and ready to fight."

Great Ajax spoke without knowing his fate following the funeral games held to honor Achilles.

Diomedes replied, "Of course, we should obey the will of the gods. If Thetis wants us to compete in funeral games, then we ought to do that and not fight the Trojans. In addition, we ought to honor Achilles ourselves in addition to the immortals honoring Achilles."

Thetis came out of the sea and approached the Greeks, some of whom were eager to compete in the funeral games, although most were happy simply to watch the games. Thetis, who was wearing a dark veil, brought out the prizes for the games. The Greeks were eager to start the games.

Before the athletic games began, Nestor gave a funeral oration. In public speaking, Nestor was the clear superior among all the Greeks. Even Odysseus, a master of rhetoric, acknowledged that Nestor, the much older man, was his superior in public speaking. So did Agamemnon, the leader of all the Greeks fighting against Troy.

Nestor praised Thetis, the most beautiful and intelligent of all the sea-nymphs. Thetis was delighted by the praise. Nestor told the story of Thetis' wedding, which took place on Mount Pelion near the cave of Chiron, the wise Centaur. Nestor spoke of the immortals who all attended the wedding, and of the Horae bringing and serving immortal food, and of Themis, the goddess of divine law, laughing as she set out silver tables, and of Hephaestus, the blacksmith god, building a fire, and of nymphs mixing ambrosia in gold chalices, and of the Graces entertaining with dance, and of the Muses entertaining with song, and of how the hills, rivers, wild animals, and sky rejoiced with the immortals and the mortals.

Nestor also praised the deeds of glorious Achilles. He spoke of the twelve cities that Achilles had conquered by sea, of the eleven that Achilles had conquered on land, of how Achilles had wounded Telephus, of how Achilles had killed Eetion while conquering the city of Thebe, of how Achilles had killed Cycnus, Polydorus, Troilus, and Asteropaeus, of how Achilles had dammed the water of the Xanthus River with the corpses of Trojans and their allies and had made the water of the river red with their blood and had killed Lycaon by the river, and of how Achilles had killed Hector, Penthesilea, and Memnon, who was the son of the goddess Dawn. Nestor also spoke of Achilles' great size, strength, and speed, and of how handsome Achilles was and how fearsome in battle. Finally, he prayed that the Greeks would find another Achilles in Neoptolemus, Achilles' son who would soon arrive at Troy after journeying from the island of Scyros.

The Greeks shouted their pleasure at the speech of Nestor, and Thetis, who was also pleased, gave him the horses that Telephus had given to Achilles. Before the Greeks sailed to Troy, they got off course and went to Mysia, a country against which they made war. Achilles wounded Telephus, the king of Mysia, in the thigh. The wound would not heal, and Telephus consulted the oracle of Delphi, who told him, "He who wounded shall heal." Achilles healed the wound using rust from the head of the spear that had caused the wound, and in return Telephus gave Achilles some horses and told the Greeks how to get to Troy. Those were the horses that Thetis awarded to Nestor, whose aides took them to his camp.

The first athletic game was the footrace, and Thetis set out as the prize for the winner ten cows, each of which was suckling a calf. Achilles had won these animals in a raid on Mount Ida.

Two men rose to compete in the footrace: Teucer and Little Ajax. They did not compete naked, as was the custom. Instead, because Thetis and other goddesses were present, the Greek athletes wore clothing that covered up their sex organs. Agamemnon showed the racers where they would race, and Eris, the goddess of discord, urged them to run quickly. Teucer and Little Ajax did run quickly. The race was close until a god or a mischievous spirit made Teucer trip on the root of a tamarisk close to the finish line. His left ankle twisted, and the veins swelled. Little Ajax raced past him and won the cows and their calves. Teucer, helped by friends, limped to doctors, who bandaged his ankle and stopped the pain.

The next event was wrestling. The competitors were Diomedes and Great Ajax, who attacked each other like wild, hungry, carnivorous beasts fighting over the carcass of a stag. Diomedes and Great Ajax were both strong and deadly, and they kicked up dust as they wrestled. Great Ajax grabbed Diomedes and tried to break his ribs, but Diomedes lifted Great Ajax and then threw him to the ground and sat on him.

Great Ajax was angry at being bested in the first round. Determined to win the second round, he covered his hands with dust to soak up the sweat, and then he and Diomedes fought like two bulls fighting on a mountain. The necks and backs of Diomedes and Great Ajax cracked with the effort that the two men made. Diomedes grabbed Great Ajax' thighs but could not knock him to the ground. Great Ajax grabbed Diomedes' shoulders but could not push him to the ground. Finally, Great Ajax grabbed Diomedes' torso and threw him on the ground.

The two wrestlers were ready and eager to compete in a third round, but Nestor told them, "This is enough wrestling. You two, now that Achilles is dead, have shown that you are our best wrestlers by far." The two wrestlers kissed in accordance with the ancient custom; the wrestling competition ended with friendship.

Thetis gave the two wrestlers four slave-women who were intelligent and skilled in crafts. Only Briseis surpassed them. Achilles had made these women slaves when he conquered the city of Lesbos, and they served at meals. The first served the food, the second poured the wine, the third poured water so the diners could wash their hands, and the last removed the tables after the meal. Diomedes and Great Ajax divided the women and sent them to their ships.

The next contest was boxing. Idomeneus stood up to compete; he was skilled in athletic contests, although his hair was partially gray. No one challenged him because of his skill and because he was an older man. Thetis gave him the horses and chariot that Patroclus had taken after he had killed Sarpedon, the son of Zeus. Idomeneus won the prize without having to compete and to bleed.

Phoenix spoke, "By the will of the gods, Idomeneus has won this prize, which is right: An older man has been honored. But now you younger men need to hold a boxing contest. Box to honor Achilles."

The younger men stayed quiet and did not volunteer, and Nestor said to them, "You younger men fight in battle, and so you should not avoid a boxing match. Younger men should enjoy boxing; a boxing match is a time and place to win glory. I wish that I were young again. I competed in the funeral games that my cousin Acastus held to honor his father, Pelias. I boxed Polydeuces to a draw, and we each won equal prizes. I won the prize for wrestling without having to compete because everyone was afraid of me. Even Ancaeus would not wrestle me. I had defeated him previously while I was among the Epeans. I am old now, but you are still young, and so you ought to compete in a boxing match."

Epeus, who would soon build the Trojan Horse, stood up. He was a good boxer, although he was not a good warrior. For a while, it seemed that no one would challenge Epeus and he would win the prize without competing, but then Acamas, the son of Theseus, challenged him.

The two boxers wore pieces of leather to protect their hands, and first they swung their arms and moved them and tested them to see if they were warmed up for boxing. As Epeus and Acamas boxed, their friends cheered them. For a while, they watched each other and then suddenly they fought. Blood flowed and mixed with sweat to form a red froth. Epeus steadily threw blows at Acamas, but Acamas was skilled enough to avoid many of the blows, causing them to hit only empty air. Acamas then hit Epeus' brow and cut it to the bone. The blood flowed as Epeus retaliated by hitting Acamas' temple and knocking him to the ground. Acamas immediately stood up again and hit Epeus' head. Epeus retaliated with a left to Acamas' brow and a right to Acamas' nose. Both Epeus and Acamas wanted to continue fighting, but the Greeks stopped the boxing match.

Epeus and Acamas kissed each other in friendship, and Thetis gave them each a mixing bowl made of silver. Achilles had received these bowls from Euneus, the son of Jason the Argonaut. Euneus had ransomed the Trojan Lycaon, whom Achilles had captured. Hephaestus had originally made the bowls and given them to the god Dionysus when Dionysus brought his bride, Ariadne, to Mount Olympus, after Jason had — involuntarily — left her behind on the island of Dia, which is now called Naxos. Dionysus had later filled the bowls with nectar and given them to Thoas, his son, who later gave them to Hypsipyle, Queen of Lemnos, who gave them to Euneus, her son, who gave them to Achilles as the ransom for Lycaon.

The physician Podalirius quickly healed the wounds of Epeus and Acamas. He sucked out the blood from the wounds, stitched the wounds, and put a salve on them. His father, the great healer Asclepius, had given him the salve, which healed even incurable wounds in only one day. The salve also took away the pain of Epeus and Acamas.

The next contest was archery. Teucer and Little Ajax, who had previously competed against each other in the footrace, again competed against each other. Teucer was a talented archer who came from the island of Salamis; Little Ajax was the best of the archers from Locris.

The target was a helmet with a horsehair crest, which Agamemnon set far away from the archers. Agamemnon told Teucer and Little Ajax, "The archer who shoots the arrow that cuts off the horsehair crest will be the winner."

Little Ajax shot first, and quickly. His arrow hit the helmet and made it ring. Teucer then shot. His arrow cut off the helmet's horsehair crest. Teucer's ankle had been injured in the footrace, and it still hurt, but Teucer won the archery competition and his fellow Greeks praised him.

Thetis awarded Teucer the armor of Troilus, whom Achilles had killed. Troilus had been a young, unmarried son of Hecuba, Queen of Troy, and she mourned his death. Troilus, the handsomest of her unmarried sons, was like a poppy cut by a scythe in a field before it has lived a life to maturity and produced seeds. Achilles killed Troilus before Troilus had grown a beard and had won a wife who would bear children. Troilus had gone to war as a young man — young men are bold in battle and display courage.

The next contest involved throwing a huge mass of metal. Only one warrior — Great Ajax — was strong enough to throw it, and he threw it as if it were a dry branch of an oak tree that lay in a field where reapers work and a reaper tosses the branch out of the way. As for the other Greeks, it took two men — working hard — to even lift it. In the old days, Antaeus used to throw it as a form of exercise before Heracles killed him. Antaeus was a half-giant who would regain his strength each time he touched the ground. Heracles battled him and kept throwing him to the ground, but he discovered that Antaeus kept regaining his strength, so to kill Antaeus, Heracles lifted him off the ground and strangled him. After killing Antaeus, Heracles took the huge mass of metal and other booty. Heracles later gave the metal to Telamon, the king of Salamis, after they had conquered the city of Troy a generation before the generation that was fighting the Trojan War, and Telamon gave it to his son, Great Ajax, to take to Troy.

Thetis awarded Great Ajax the armor of Memnon, the Ethiopian king whom Achilles had killed. Memnon had been massive, and his armor was massive. Great Ajax was the only Greek whom the armor would fit, and Great Ajax laughed with pleasure as he received the prize.

The next contest was the broad jump. Many warriors competed, and Agapenor easily defeated the other competitors. Thetis gave him the armor of Cycnus, who had killed Protesilaus, the first Greek to be killed at Troy. Cycnus had killed many more Greeks, and after Achilles killed him, the Trojans mourned.

The next contest was javelin throwing. Euryalus easily defeated the other competitors, and the Greeks did not think that even an arrow could surpass his throw. Thetis gave him a large silver bowl that Achilles had won when he killed Mynes during the sack of the city of Lyrnessus.

The next contest was a fight while using hands and feet. Great Ajax stood up and challenged all the other Greeks to fight him. Great Ajax was so strong that no one accepted his challenge; Great Ajax' fists could crush a warrior's face. The Greeks nodded at Euryalus, inviting him — an expert fighter — to accept Great Ajax' challenge, but Euryalus said, "Friends, I will accept the challenge of any warrior except Great Ajax, who is by far superior to me. If he were to get angry during the fight, he could kill me. Even if he doesn't get angry during the fight, I do not think that I would be able to walk back to my ship after the fight."

The other Greeks laughed, and Great Ajax was pleased with the praise. Great Ajax did not have to fight anyone to win. Thetis gave him two talents of silver. She looked at Great Ajax, was reminded of Achilles, her son, and felt sad.

The next event was the chariot race. Menelaus, Eurypylus, Eumelus, Thoas, and Polypoetes prepared their horses and chariots and drove them to the starting point. The horses were ready, and their ears pricked up. Then the horses raced, speeding away like Harpies. Dust rose in the air like smoke or fog.

Eumelus jumped out in front, and Thoas was a close second, but Menelaus won the race — Thoas and Eurypylus were both thrown from their chariots during the race.

Menelaus' ancestor, Pelops, had won an important chariot race so that he could marry Hippodamia, the daughter of Oenomaus, King of Pisa. Oenomaus worried about a prophecy that his son-in-law would kill him, so he challenged all suitors of Hippodamia to a chariot race. The agreement was that if the suitor won, the suitor would marry Hippodamia, but if the suitor lost, Oenomaus would cut off the suitor's head and display it on his chariot. Pelops won the chariot race — Oenomaus died during the race when his chariot's wheels came off — and married Hippodamia. Menelaus' horses were faster than the horses of Pelops.

Doctors attended to the wounds of Thoas and Eurypylus, and Thetis gave Menelaus a gold goblet that had belonged to King Eetion. Achilles had won it when he sacked Thebe, the city of King Eetion.

The next contest was a horserace. The horses were eager to run; they pounded the earth with their feet and they champed the bits of the bridles. Several riders competed. Sthenelus rode a fast but undisciplined horse that frequently got off the racecourse. The horse came from the stock of Arion, whose father was Zephyrus, the god of the West wind. Arion used to race his father. The gods had given Arion to Adrastus, King of Argos, who gave one of Arion's foals to Diomedes, who had married one of his daughters. Diomedes had given the offspring of Arion to his friend Sthenelus, who finished in second place in the horserace because of the wildness of his horse. Agamemnon finished in first place. The Greeks honored both men. Agamemnon had finished first, but Sthenelus' horse was faster. Thetis gave Agamemnon the silver breastplate that Achilles had taken from Polydorus, and she gave Sthenelus the helmet that had belonged to Asteropaeus, two spears, and a belt.

Thetis gave prizes to the other horsemen and to all of those who had competed in the funeral games. Odysseus was unhappy. He liked prizes, but he had been wounded in battle while helping to defend Achilles' corpse and had been unable to compete.

Chapter 5: The Madness of Great Ajax

Thetis then brought out the divine armor that Hephaestus had made for her son. The armor gleamed; the decorations that Hephaestus had put on the shield especially gleamed.

Hephaestus had put on the shield the sky and the sea and the land. He had put on the shield the winds and the clouds and the Moon and the Sun and the constellations. He had put on the shield Tethys, the mother of all rivers, and Oceanus, the god of the river Ocean that surrounds all land.

Hephaestus had put on the shield birds, lions, jackals, bears, leopards, boars, and hunters and their dogs. All looked as if they were alive.

Hephaestus had put on the shield battles in which were warriors and horses. In the battle, the gods Terror and Dread were active, as were Eris and the Furies and the Fates. From each warrior, sweat and blood dripped to the ground.

Hephaestus had put on the shield Gorgons with snakes in their hair.

In addition to these scenes of war, Hephaestus had put on the shield scenes of peace. He put on the shield scenes of civilization and Lady Justice. Inside a city, people worked at various tasks. Outside the city, farmers grew crops.

Hephaestus had put on the shield the steep mountain of Virtue, on top of which was the goddess of Virtue, standing on the top of a palm tree, her head disappearing into the sky. Paths led to the top of the mountain, but the mountain was very difficult to climb and few people attempted the climb to the top.

Hephaestus had put on the shield reapers of grain who wielded sickles. Other workers bound the sheaves of grain. Some oxen hauled wagonloads of sheaves to barns. Some oxen plowed the fields.

Hephaestus had put on the shield a celebration with flutes and lyres and dances and feasts. Near the dancing, Aphrodite arose from the sea. Sea-foam clung to her hair, and her attendants were winged Desire, who smiled, and the Graces.

Hephaestus had put on the shield Thetis' marriage to Peleus. She and her sister sea-nymphs arose from the sea. All feasted on Mount Pelion. Around the feast were meadows, flowers, groves of trees, and springs of water.

Hephaestus had put on the shield sailors at sea during a storm. Ships were in distress, and sailors were scared. Some sailors manned the sails, while other sailors pulled hard at the oars. The oars disturbed the water and made it white.

Hephaestus had put on the shield the beings of the sea, including Poseidon. Smiling, he rode his chariot on the sea and whipped his horses and calmed the waves. Dolphins swam alongside Poseidon's chariot.

Hephaestus had put on the shield many other things. All along the outside of the rim Hephaestus had put the river Ocean.

Thetis now put down beside the shield Achilles' divinely made helmet. Hephaestus had put on the helmet an image of Zeus looking very angry. Zeus and the other gods were fighting the rebelling Titans. Zeus threw a constant barrage of thunderbolts at the Titans, who were surrounded by fire.

Thetis placed beside the helmet Achilles' divinely made breastplate and greaves. Achilles found the greaves to be light, but all other warriors thought the greaves were heavy. Thetis also lay down Achilles' divinely made sword, gold sword-belt, and silver scabbard. She also lay down Achilles' spear, which still bore traces of the blood of Hector.

Thetis then said to the Greeks, "The funeral games and athletic contests are over, but I have a reward for the warrior who kept the Trojans from taking the body of my son. I want to reward the man who recovered my son's body so that we could give it a proper burial; that man is the best of the Greeks. Will that man come forward, please? To him I will give Achilles' armor and weapons."

Not one, but two, warriors stood up. This would be a contest.

Looking down from Mount Olympus, Zeus thought, *This is interesting. I don't think that Thetis believed that this would turn into a contest. I think that she believed that one man — Great Ajax — obviously did the most to keep the Trojans from taking possession of the corpse of Achilles.*

Odysseus and Great Ajax were the two warriors who stood up and claimed the prize. Great Ajax, tallest of all the Greek warriors, looked like the evening star — the star that outshines all other stars at night. Great Ajax asked that Idomeneus, Nestor, and Agamemnon judge who had done the most to recover the corpse of Achilles and is therefore the best of the Greeks. Great Ajax regarded these three men as expert judges; he knew that they had witnessed his deeds. Odysseus also regarded them as expert judges who were fair and incorruptible.

Idomeneus and Agamemnon were happy to serve as judges, but Nestor took them aside and spoke to them in private: "Let's think about this contest, which I fear will be a disaster for the Greeks. Only one warrior can be awarded Achilles' armor and weapons. That warrior will be happy, but the other warrior will be very unhappy and will blame us and all the other Greeks for what he will think is an insult. I predict that that warrior will stay away from the battles and not fight for us. Great Ajax and Odysseus are both very important to our cause. Great Ajax is a great warrior, while Odysseus has a great intellect.

"Listen to me: an old man who has gained wisdom through experience. A knowledgeable old man is wiser than a knowledgeable young man because the old man has experienced more. Let us three not judge the contest. Let the Trojans do it. They can decide which warrior they are most afraid of and which warrior did the most to recover the corpse of Achilles. We have many Trojans in our camp whom we are holding for ransom or are holding until we can sell them as slaves. These Trojans will make a fair judgment. They will not have a favorite because they hate all Greeks. If we do this, we may be able to avoid a disaster.

"If all goes well, the loser of this contest will become angry at the Trojans, not at us. If all goes well, the loser of this contest will fight more fiercely on the battlefield."

Looking down from Mount Olympus, Zeus thought, *This is interesting. The contest has changed. Thetis said that she wanted to give to the divine armor to the Greek warrior who had recovered the corpse of Achilles; she regards that warrior as being the best of the Greeks. But now the contest includes a decision about whom the Trojans fear most. This could benefit Odysseus. His intelligence and ability to form plots pose a clear danger to the Trojans, and they know it.*

Agamemnon listened carefully, and then he said, "Nestor, no one here — whether old or young — is wiser than you are. You can see ahead and determine whether problems can arise. Only you saw the problem that could arise from this contest. Your advice is good, and I will accept it. If a warrior finds fault in whatever judgment the Trojan captives make, that warrior will direct his anger at the Trojan captives and not at us."

Idomeneus, Nestor, and Agamemnon then publicly declined to judge the contest, and some Trojans were brought out to listen to speeches by Great Ajax and Odysseus and decide the winner. The contest would be like a trial. Both men would speak, and then both men would make shorter additional speeches.

Great Ajax, who was annoyed that Idomeneus, Nestor, and Agamemnon would not judge the contest, spoke first: "Odysseus, you are intelligent, but intelligence is not the same thing as strength in battle. Are you really saying that you did the most to keep the Trojans from taking away the corpse of Achilles? I am the one who killed Trojans while you stayed away. You are weak and cowardly. You compared to me are like a dog compared to a lion. You lack courage in battle. Instead, your strength lies in tricks and plots."

Zeus thought, *Not everything Great Ajax said is true, although some of it is. Odysseus did help Great Ajax to keep the Trojans from taking away the corpse of Achilles, although clearly Great Ajax did the most to protect Achilles' corpse. It is true that Odysseus' strength is forming plots, but Odysseus is also a good warrior. Great Ajax is being way too critical of Odysseus.*

Great Ajax continued, "Here is some evidence that you lack courage. You did not want to fight at Troy. You thought up a trick that you hoped would keep you out of the fighting. You pretended to be insane, and you sowed your fields with salt. Palamedes knew that you were faking insanity, and he placed your infant son, Telemachus, in front of the plow. If you were insane, you would kill your son. But, of course, you were faking insanity and you turned the plow aside and did not kill your son. You then had to come to Troy and fight — against your will.

"You have done great evil in your life, Odysseus. A poisonous snake on the island of Lemnos bit Philoctetes. The wound stank and caused Philoctetes to have fits, and you persuaded the Greeks to leave him on the island.

"And rumor has it that you brought about the death of Palamedes by hiding gold in his tent along with a letter purportedly written by Priam, King of Troy. Rumor has it that you did these things to make it look like Palamedes was a traitor to us Greeks. Palamedes was executed.

"Who is the better warrior: you or I? I once saved your life on the battlefield. You were wounded, and many Trojan warriors fought you. Other Greek warriors were not near you. You cried for help, and I came and rescued you. You went back to the Greek camp until your wound healed. If not for me, you would have died on the battlefield. Since you are now saying that you did the most to keep the Trojans from taking the corpse of Achilles, I wish that you had died on the battlefield that day. The Trojans should have fed your body to the dogs."

Zeus thought, *This contest is going to end badly. Great Ajax is so angry that he is saying things that he ought not to say.*

Great Ajax continued, "Odysseus, you say that you are the best warrior of the Greeks, but why then do you keep your ships in the middle of the Greek camps? Achilles had his ships and I have my ships at the far sides of the Greek camps. Those are the most vulnerable places, and those are the places where the mightiest warriors are needed to protect the Greek camps.

"I am the warrior who did the most to keep the fire away from the Greeks ships when the Trojans stormed our defensive trench and wall and fought at the ships. Hector managed to burn only one ship. You did not fight Hector; I did. You were afraid of Hector; I was not."

Zeus thought, *Great Ajax did fight magnificently when Hector brought fire to the Greek ships. However, Great Ajax did not mention that Odysseus was wounded at that time and unable to fight.*

Great Ajax continued, "I was the one who picked up Achilles' corpse and carried it back to our camp. You are hoping to win this contest with your words. What you lack in skill with weapons, you make up for in skill in rhetoric. But if you should win this contest, you can't wear Achilles' armor; it is too big for you. I can wear Achilles' armor; it fits me, and I won't shame the gods when I wear it.

"I don't see why we are talking here. This ought to be a contest of strength, not of words. Thetis wants the strongest warrior to have her son's armor, not the warrior who speaks best in a council.

"In addition, I ought to have the armor because I have some of the same ancestors as Achilles. My father is Telamon, whose father is Aeacus, whose father is Zeus. Achilles' father is Peleus, whose father is Aeacus, whose father is Zeus."

Odysseus then spoke: "You have said many words, but the content of your words is lacking. I am far your superior in making plans and speeches, and these abilities are valuable. Skill and intelligence multiply strength, as we see when quarrymen cut out blocks of stone from a cliff that seems unbreakable, as we see when sailors cross a dangerous sea, as we see when hunters kill lions, leopards, boars, and other dangerous wild beasts, and as we see when men use powerful oxen to pull a plow. Intelligence accomplishes everything. A smart man is always better than a stupid man.

"When Diomedes volunteered to make a night raid against the Trojans after we Greeks had lost a battle, he selected me to go with him because I am intelligent. He did not select you, although he had that option. Diomedes and I killed many Trojan allies, including King Rhesus, and we stole his horses. We succeeded in raising the morale of the Greeks despite the previous day's defeat in battle.

"Because I am intelligent, I was able to have Achilles come to Troy to fight in the war. I persuaded him with words."

Zeus thought, *Odysseus is using rhetoric well. He is not going into detail about how he persuaded Achilles to come to Troy to fight in the war because it would put Achilles and Thetis in a bad light and he does not want to upset Thetis. Thetis did not want Achilles to go to the Trojan War because she knew that he would die there; therefore, she disguised him as a girl and hid him in the court of King Lycomedes on the island of Scyros. Odysseus showed the girls much fine women's clothing, among which he had placed some weapons. The fine clothing fascinated the girls, but the weapons fascinated the disguised Achilles. Having penetrated Achilles' disguise, Odysseus forced him to fight at Troy.*

Odysseus continued, "Strength is nothing without intelligence. Fortunately, the gods gave me both strength and intelligence.

"You did not say the truth when you said that you saved my life on the battlefield. Although I was wounded, I did not run away from the Trojans; instead, I held my ground and killed many Trojans. You looked after yourself, not me, and you ran away."

Zeus thought, *Odysseus is correct when he said that he killed many Trojans although he was wounded, but he is completely wrong when he said that Great Ajax did not save his life but instead ran away. Odysseus killed many Trojans; he fought hard to save his own life. But he needed help, he called for help, and Great Ajax and Menelaus rescued him and fought the Trojans and allowed Odysseus to go back to the Greek ships.*

Odysseus continued, "You pointed out that my ships are in the middle and not on the sides of the Greek camps. There is a reason for that. My ships are in the middle so that I am available to make plans with Agamemnon and

Menelaus. The advice I give them is good. I did not put my ships in the middle because of cowardice.

"I showed that I have courage when I disguised myself as a beggar, including whipping myself to inflict wounds, so that I could go into Troy as a spy and find out what they were planning to do. Helen recognized me, but I was able to leave Troy safely, although I had to kill Trojans as I left the city.

"I was not afraid of Hector. When he challenged any of the Greeks to fight him in single combat, I was one of the first to volunteer to fight him."

Zeus thought, *Odysseus is guilty of the fallacy of suppressed evidence here: What he said is true, but he is leaving out some information. No one at first was willing to fight Hector in single combat. It took Nestor to shame the Greeks so that some of them would volunteer to fight him. Both Great Ajax and Odysseus volunteered, among others, and a lottery resulted in Great Ajax fighting Hector. In the single combat, which darkness ended before anyone was killed, Great Ajax got the better of Hector.*

Odysseus continued, "Who did the most to recover the corpse of Achilles? I did. I killed more of the enemy than you did, and I was wounded as I fought.

"I have one more reason why I should be awarded Achilles' armor. He and I are both descended from Zeus. The father of my grandfather Autolycus was Hermes, and Hermes is the son of Zeus."

Great Ajax then responded to Odysseus' speech: "You are annoying, Odysseus. Who did the most to recover the corpse of Achilles? I did. I am the one who made the Trojans grow weak in the knees when they saw me. I am the one who kept attacking them, and I am the one who made them flee. I was like an eagle attacking geese that are feeding in a field by a river. To escape my spear, the Trojans fled and hid behind the walls of Troy. Were you fighting by the side of the corpse of Achilles? If you were, I did not see you. If you were fighting, you were fighting at a distance from the corpse of Achilles."

Zeus thought, *Odysseus did fight, and he was close to the corpse of Achilles, but Great Ajax clearly did the most to keep the Trojans from taking the corpse of Achilles. Both Great Ajax and Odysseus are exaggerating or even lying in their speeches.*

Odysseus replied to Great Ajax' speech, "You are a great warrior, but I do not think that I am your inferior in either strength or intelligence. In fact, I think that when it comes to intelligence, I am your superior by far. We may be equal in strength, or I may be slightly stronger than you. Remember that at the funeral games held to honor Patroclus, we wrestled and you were unable to defeat me; I was slightly your better."

Zeus thought, *The wrestling match ended in a draw, although Odysseus was, as he said, slightly Great Ajax' better. But Odysseus' slight superiority came from his knowledge of wrestling moves, not from any supposed superior strength.*

The Trojan captives then made their decision: They decided — unanimously — that Odysseus deserved the divinely made armor of Achilles. The Greeks groaned: They thought that Great Ajax deserved the armor. Odysseus was thrilled with his victory.

Zeus thought, *This is interesting. What is going on here? Perhaps the Trojan captives are intelligent enough to try to cause dissension among the Greeks. Clearly, Great Ajax did the most to keep the Trojans from Achilles' corpse and armor, and yet the Trojan captives decided unanimously to give Achilles' armor to Odysseus. Maybe they are valuing intelligence over strength, or maybe they want to cause a quarrel between Great Ajax and Odysseus. Nestor hoped to avoid trouble by having the Trojan captives judge this contest. Sorry, Nestor — it didn't work.*

Great Ajax was shocked by the decision. His heart and his head hurt. He stared at the ground; he could not understand how the Trojan captives had made such a decision. Friends led him to his ships and tried to comfort him with words.

The Greeks began to prepare their meal, and Thetis and the sea-nymphs returned to the sea. The Nereids — the daughters of the minor sea-god Nereus — were angry at Prometheus, who had told Zeus that Thetis would give birth to a son who would be greater than his father. This information had caused Zeus to marry Thetis against her will to a mortal. Zeus did not want a god to sleep with Thetis; their son might be powerful enough to overthrow Zeus and become the new king of gods and mortals.

The sea-nymph Cymothoe said, "Because Prometheus is the reason Zeus married Thetis to a mortal against her will, he deserved the punishment he received, even if he received it for the wrong reason. Because Prometheus had given the knowledge of how to use fire to mortals, Zeus caused him to be chained to a rock. Each day, an eagle ate Prometheus' liver, which grew back so that it could be eaten again the next day."

The Greeks ate their meal and drank wine and slept, but Great Ajax did not eat or drink or sleep. Angry at his fellow Greeks, he put on his armor, held his sword, and brooded. What ought he to do? Set fire to the ships and kill all the Greeks? Or kill only Odysseus?

Athena especially respected Odysseus because he was good at forming plans like she was. She also liked the many sacrifices that he had made to her. She did not want Great Ajax to kill him, so she made Great Ajax insane.

Great Ajax was like a storm in his madness. He rushed around like a wild animal that foams at the mouth and thinks about killing hunting dogs and the hunters who have killed the animal's cubs. The animal rushes around, searching for its cubs, and it fights any dogs or hunters it sees. Great Ajax' spirit was like the boiling water in a cauldron. He raged like a hurricane or a forest fire. He cried out, and all who saw or heard him trembled.

Dawn arrived, and Hera met the god Sleep, and she kissed him. Hera had bribed Sleep with a marriage to the young Grace Pasithea to put Zeus to sleep after Hera had slept with Zeus. This allowed Poseidon to help the Greeks fight the Trojans although Zeus had forbidden such interference. Hera's interference harmed Zeus and the Trojans, and Athena's interference was harming Great Ajax and the Greeks.

Great Ajax killed many sheep, thinking that he was killing Odysseus and other Greeks.

Menelaus quickly learned of Great Ajax' madness and said to Agamemnon, privately, "We will suffer much today. Soon, Great Ajax in his madness will set our ships on fire and then kill all of us because of the contest over Achilles' armor. I wish that Thetis had never brought the armor out to give away, and I wish that Odysseus had not challenged Great Ajax for the armor. Clearly, Great Ajax is the stronger warrior. We have behaved foolishly, and the gods must be against us. With Achilles dead, Great Ajax is our strongest warrior and our best hope of defeating the Trojans. But now the gods seem determined to destroy Great Ajax and us, too."

Agamemnon replied, "Blame the gods, not Odysseus, who has served us well. I do not hold Odysseus responsible for what is happening."

As Great Ajax killed sheep, the shepherds hid, trying to avoid being killed. They were like rabbits hiding in thick brush from eagles.

After Great Ajax had killed a ram, he said to it, "Lie there dead, Odysseus. The armor of Achilles is of no use to you. You will never see your wife again, or your son, or your parents. You will never take care of your parents in their old age. You have died in a land far from your home, and the dogs and birds will eat your flesh."

Athena then took away Great Ajax' madness, and he realized that he had been killing sheep and not Odysseus and other Greeks.

Great Ajax looked around, and he realized what had happened: The gods or a god had tricked him. He stood still; he could not move. At first he could not talk because of his misery, but then he said, "Why do the gods hate me? Why do the gods treat me this way? They made me insane and made me kill sheep. I wanted and I want to kill Odysseus. He is the evil one, and I wish that the Furies would pursue and exact vengeance on him. I also wish that the Furies would pursue other Greeks, including Agamemnon. I hope that Agamemnon will never return happily to his home in Greece.

"Why am I still alive? Why am I in this army of Greeks? Why live a life that is not worth living? I am a brave man, but my bravery is not recognized. The man who gets honor is the worse man. The Greeks honor Odysseus, and the Greeks forget all the acts of courage that I have done in this war."

Great Ajax had previously fought Hector in single combat. Because of darkness, the single combat had been stopped, and he and Hector had exchanged gifts that showed that they respected each other's courage and strength. Great Ajax had given Hector a sword-belt, and Hector had given Great Ajax a sword.

Great Ajax now cut his throat with the sword that Hector had given him. His blood gushed out, and Great Ajax fell to the ground and died.

The Greeks had stayed away from Great Ajax when he was insane because they were afraid of him. Now they came to him and mourned his death. They poured dust on their heads. When men take away lambs to butcher for a meal, the ewes bleat in anguish. The Greeks cried out in anguish for the death of Great Ajax.

Teucer, Great Ajax' half-brother — both were the sons of Telamon, but they had different mothers — wanted to kill himself out of grief, but the other Greeks stopped him. Teucer grieved the way that a child grieves when he becomes an orphan. His mother has died, and he has never known his father.

Teucer said, "For what purpose did you kill yourself? Did you kill yourself so that the Trojans can kill the Greeks? Now that you are dead, the Greeks will not be able to fight courageously in battle. You were our strongest and most courageous warrior.

"Now that you are dead, I wish to die here, far from home. I want to be buried here with you. I care more about you than I do about my parents, whom I do not know whether they are still alive on the island of Salamis."

Tecmessa, the spear-bride of Great Ajax, mourned his death. He had treated her as if she were his lawfully wedded wife, and she had given birth in his camp to his still-small son, who was named Eurysaces.

Tecmessa said, "I did not expect that you would die here at Troy, and now that you are dead, I am wretched. I wish that I had died before you died. This day is worse than the day that I became a slave with other captured women when you dragged me away from my home and my parents. I had been a queen, and you made me a slave. But you made me your spear-bride, and you treated me well. You promised that when you returned to Salamis that you would make me its queen, but now that will never happen. And your son will never have a father to care for him, and he will never succeed you as king of Salamis. Instead, your son will be a slave and miserable, and I will be a slave and miserable. All of this will happen because you are now dead."

Agamemnon comforted her: "Tecmessa, you will not become a slave — not as long as Teucer and I still live. We still respect you and your son, just as we respected you and your son while Great Ajax was still living. We wish that he were still alive. The entire Trojan army was unable to kill him. Only he was able to bring about his own death."

All the Greeks mourned, including Odysseus, who said, "Anger is a great evil, and because of his anger at me, Great Ajax killed himself. I wish that the Trojans had not awarded me Achilles' armor. Because they did, Great Ajax killed himself. I am not responsible for his anger or for his death. Fate is responsible. If I had known that this would happen, I would never have challenged him for the armor of Achilles. I would have given him the armor and whatever other gifts he desired. I did not know that this would happen. We argued not over a wife or a city or great wealth and possessions. We argued over ability and prowess. Sensible men should be able to argue over such things without it ending like this."

Nestor then said, "We have suffered much. Great Ajax is dead. Achilles is dead. My own son Antilochus is dead. But we cannot mourn forever. We must respect the dead by giving the dead a proper funeral. That is the best thing that we can do for the dead."

The Greeks carried the corpse of Great Ajax to the ships, and they cleaned his corpse and covered it with cloth. They built a funeral pyre and burned his body with many sheep and robes and cattle and horses and gold and armor and amber.

Amber originated from grief. When Phaëthon demanded proof that Helios, the Sun-god, was his father, he made Helios swear an inviolable oath that he would grant Phaëthon a wish. After Helios made the inviolable oath, Phaëthon demanded that he be allowed to drive the Sun-chariot that brought light to earth. Phaëthon could not control the horses, and he nearly destroyed the earth, and Zeus was forced to save the earth by throwing a thunderbolt at Phaëthon and killing him so that Helios could drive the Sun-chariot. Helios' daughters cried tears, and Helios turned those tears into amber.

Along with amber, the Greeks also burned ivory and silver and jars filled with oil and other good things in honor of Great Ajax.

Thetis sent a strong wind to assist in the burning of the corpse of Great Ajax. Smoke rose from the funeral pyre just as smoke rose from the thunderbolts that Zeus threw when he fought and defeated the giant Enceladus or just as smoke rose from the fire that the living Heracles lit when the Centaur Nessus tricked Heracles' wife, Deianira, into giving Heracles a robe soaked in Nessus' blood, which burned Heracles like acid and caused him to burn himself to death and to become a god.

From the walls of their city, the Trojans watched the funeral pyre burn. The Trojans rejoiced; the Greeks mourned.

When the fire burned down, the Greeks put it out with wine. They gathered Great Ajax' bones and put them in a box made of gold. The Greeks heaped a great mound of earth over the bones and then went to their ships and ate.

The Greeks found it difficult to sleep that night because they were afraid that the Trojans might attack them now that Great Ajax was dead.

Chapter 6: Eurypylus Comes to Troy

Dawn arrived, and Menelaus held an assembly of all the Greeks. He intended to test the army's morale by suggesting that they give up and go home, and he hoped that they would reject the suggestion. He said to them, "I am discouraged because so many of you Greeks have died for me before the walls of Troy. So many Greeks will not return home and take care of their aged parents. The gods have opposed us and brought death to many of us. Can any of us take joy in battle under such circumstances? Let us return home — now! Great Ajax is dead. So is Achilles. If we could not conquer Troy with these warriors alive, will we be able to conquer Troy with these warriors dead? These warriors and others died for me and for Helen, my bitch of a wife. I am much more concerned about you warriors than I am about Helen. Paris can have Helen! They deserve each other! Let Priam and the Trojans have all the troubles that Helen will bring to them. Let us return to Greece and live rather than stay at Troy and die."

So Menelaus spoke, but he was actually planning how he could spill the blood of Paris and other Trojans and tear down the walls of Troy. He hoped that the Greek warriors were planning the same things.

Diomedes replied, "To leave Troy would be cowardly. You sound as if you were a child or a woman who lacks strength and courage. We Greeks will stay here and conquer Troy. And if any Greek wishes to go home, I myself will cut off his head and give it to the birds to eat. Instead of fleeing, those of us warriors who have courage will sharpen our spears and make sure our shields and other armor are ready to do their duty in battle. Let us eat and then go to war and see how courageous we are."

Calchas the prophet said, "You know that my prophecies come true. I have prophesized that Troy will fall in the tenth year of the war, and this will in fact happen. Victory will be ours. However, before the victory can occur, we must send Diomedes and Odysseus to the island of Scyros to persuade Neoptolemus, Achilles' son, to come to Troy and fight for us. Neoptolemus will help us to win the war."

The Greeks knew Calchas and believed his prophecies; they believed him when he said that Neoptolemus would help them win the war.

Odysseus said, "I will not make a long speech. When people are grieving, a speaker brings no pleasure — not even a singer whom the Muses love brings pleasure to grieving men. I pray to the gods that Diomedes and I will succeed in this task. The two of us will be able to persuade Neoptolemus to come and fight for us in this war. His mother may cry with grief as he leaves with us, but the son of a mighty warrior is a warrior, too, and he will come with us."

Menelaus then said to Odysseus, "You have done good work for us Greeks. Tell Neoptolemus that if he fights for us in this war that I will give him in marriage my daughter, Hermione, along with many gifts. He should be happy and proud to marry my daughter and be allied with my family."

The council ended, the men ate, and Diomedes and Odysseus set sail with twenty men to row. The men worked hard at the oars, just as oxen work hard at dragging a wagon, and the ship sped swiftly over the sea.

The Greek warriors who stayed at the camps sharpened their weapons and prepared for battle. The Trojans also prepared for battle, and they prayed to the gods for victory.

The gods heard and answered the Trojans' prayers: They brought a mighty champion to Troy to fight for them. The King of the Cetaeans, Eurypylus, whose grandfather was Heracles, the greatest of all Greek heroes, brought an army with him to Troy. The Trojans were gladdened by the numerous reinforcements. The Trojans were like tame geese that see coming toward them the farmer who feeds them. The geese rejoice to see the farmer, and the farmer rejoices to see the geese. Trojan women stared at Eurypylus. He was the most outstanding warrior in the army that he brought with him: He was like a lion among jackals.

Paris, who had stolen Helen from Menelaus, welcomed Eurypylus. They were cousins as well as fellow warriors. Eurypylus' mother was Astyoche, the sister of Paris' father, Priam. Eurypylus' father was Telephus, whose father was Heracles and whose mother was Auge. The two had slept together without her father knowing about it. Auge's father ordered that the infant Telephus be exposed on a mountain so that he would die, but a doe that loved him as if he were her own fawn allowed him to drink milk from her udders. The children of Heracles are not meant to die in infancy.

Paris showed Eurypylus the city of Troy. He showed him the statue of Assaracus, who had ruled the city of Dardania. Assaracus' brother was Tros, an earlier king of Troy. Paris also showed him Hector's house and the shrine dedicated to the goddess Athena. Near this shrine was the home of Paris and an altar dedicated to Zeus. The two men talked, and Paris asked Eurypylus about his relatives.

When they arrived at the home of Paris, they saw Helen. Four female servants attended to her needs, and other slave-women did the tasks that female slaves do. Helen impressed Eurypylus, and Eurypylus impressed Helen. Paris and Eurypylus sat by Helen, and the three talked.

Eurypylus' army camped in front of Troy, along with many Trojan guards. His warriors unloaded their supplies and fed their horses. Night arrived, and all ate. Musicians brought out their instruments and played them. The Greeks watched and listened, and they made sure that their ships were well guarded. The Trojans and their allies were camped outside the walls of Troy, and the Greeks worried that they might make a night raid and try to set the ships on fire.

Inside the walls of Troy, Paris and Eurypylus feasted with Paris and other Trojan leaders. After the meal, Paris gave Eurypylus the best room in his home to sleep in — the room where Paris and Helen usually slept.

At dawn, Eurypylus and the other warriors armed for battle. Eurypylus' shield was magnificent — a work of art that bore images of the deeds of Eurypylus' grandfather Heracles.

Eurypylus' shield showed the infant Heracles strangling two snakes. Heracles' father was Zeus, but his mother was not Zeus' wife, Hera. Hera hated the children whom Zeus fathered outside of their marriage, and so Hera sent two snakes to strangle Heracles in his crib. But even as an infant, Heracles was immensely strong, and he strangled the two snakes. This was the first of Heracles' many deeds of courage and strength.

Eurypylus' shield showed the twelve labors of Heracles. Heracles had grown up and married Megara, and they had children, but Hera made Heracles insane and he killed his children. Heracles traveled to the oracle of Delphi to find out how he could purify himself of this evil, and the oracle told him that he had to serve Eurystheus, a king in the land of Argos, and perform ten labors for him. Heracles did this, but Eurystheus argued that two of the labors should not count, and so Heracles performed two more labors, bringing the total to twelve.

During many of his labors, Heracles killed many dangerous monsters and made the world much safer.

Eurypylus' shield showed Heracles' first labor, which was killing the Nemean lion. Heracles set out for Nemea and the lion. In Nemea, he met a shepherd named Molorchos whose son the lion had killed, and Heracles told him to wait thirty days. If Heracles returned with the carcass of the lion, then Molorchos would make a sacrifice to Zeus, but if Heracles had not returned with the lion's carcass in thirty days, that meant that Heracles was dead and Molorchos should make a sacrifice to Heracles — the Greeks sometimes made sacrifices to heroes as well as to gods. Heracles found the lion and tried to kill it by shooting arrows at it, but he discovered that weapons could not penetrate the lion's fur. Heracles forced the lion into its cave, which had two entrances. Heracles trapped the lion by blocking one entrance and then going into the cave through the other entrance. Because ordinary weapons could not penetrate the lion's skin, Heracles killed the lion by strangling it. To skin the lion, Heracles used one of the lion's claws. For the rest of his life, Heracles wore the skin of the lion. On the thirtieth day, he found Molorchos ready to make a sacrifice to Heracles, whom he thought had died, but Molorchos happily made the sacrifice to Zeus instead.

Eurypylus' shield showed Heracles' second labor, which was killing the Lernaean Hydra. In accomplishing this labor, Heracles had the help of a nephew named Iolaus. The Hydra of Lerna had nine heads, the middle of which was immortal. Heracles and Iolaus traveled to Lerna and found the Hydra's lair. Heracles forced the Hydra to leave its lair by shooting flaming arrows into the lair. Heracles fought the Hydra, but he discovered that each time a mortal head was cut off, two more heads grew in its place. Hera gave Heracles even more trouble by sending an enormous crab to fight him, but Heracles crushed the crab. Heracles then got help from Iolaus. Each time Heracles cut off one of the Hydra's mortal heads, Iolaus cauterized it with a torch, thus preventing more heads from growing. Heracles then cut off the immortal head and placed it under a boulder. The blood of the Hydra was poisonous, and before leaving, Heracles dipped the heads of his arrows into the Hydra's blood. Eurystheus, however, said that this labor did not count because Heracles had help from Iolaus in accomplishing it.

Eurypylus' shield showed Heracles' third labor, which was capturing the fire-breathing Ceryneian Hind — the goddess Artemis' golden deer that lived in Ceryneia. Eurystheus ordered Heracles to bring back this deer, whose horns were made of gold. Because the deer belonged to the goddess Artemis, Heracles did not want to kill it, so he chased it for a year — the deer was so swift that it could outrun arrows. Finally, Heracles captured the deer while it was asleep. Artemis confronted Heracles as he was taking the deer to Eurystheus, but Heracles promised to release the deer as soon as he had shown the deer to Eurystheus. Eurystheus, however, wanted the deer to be a part of his zoo — Eurystheus was hoping that Artemis would become angry at Heracles and kill him. Heracles said that Eurystheus could put the deer in his zoo, and then he released the deer, which immediately fled back to Artemis. Eurystheus complained, but Heracles said that Eurystheus should have caught the deer before it fled.

Eurypylus' shield showed Heracles' fourth labor, which was capturing the Erymanthian boar. The shield also showed Heracles' battle with the Centaurs, and his rescue of Prometheus. Boars were dangerous, and this especially dangerous boar lived on Mount Erymanthus. While traveling to Mount Erymanthus, Heracles became the guest of a Centaur named Pholus. The Centaur ate his meat raw, and Heracles ate his meat roasted. The Centaurs had a jar of wine, and Pholus and Heracles drank from it. The other Centaurs smelled the wine, and they also drank, but they did not mix the wine with water and so became drunk and unruly. Heracles fought the Centaurs and chased them, and he discovered Prometheus, who had given the knowledge of how to control fire to mortals. Zeus had punished him by chaining him to a rock on a mountain and by sending an eagle each day to eat his liver, which grew back each night so it could be eaten again the following day. Heracles shot the eagle with an arrow and released Prometheus, and then he consulted the wise Centaur Chiron, seeking advice about how to capture the Erymanthian boar. Chiron advised Heracles to drive the Erymanthian boar into deep snow and then capture it. After following Chiron's advice, Heracles took the Erymanthian boar to Eurystheus, who ordered it to be thrown into the sea. The Erymanthian boar swam to Italy, where it died. Its tusks were put on display in the temple of Apollo at Cumae.

Eurypylus' shield showed Heracles' fifth labor, which was cleaning the barn of Augeas in a single day. The cattle's manure had not been cleaned out for decades, and Augeas had hundreds of cattle. Heracles appeared before Augeas and offered to clean out his barn in one day if Augeas would give him one tenth of his cattle. Thinking that the job was impossible to accomplish in a single day, Augeas accepted the offer. Heracles opened the ends of the barn and then diverted the course of the river Alpheus so that it flowed through the barn. When the barn was cleaned out, Heracles diverted the river so that it flowed again in its original channel. Nymphs watched and marveled at this deed. Eurystheus, however, said that this labor did not count because Heracles had done it for payment.

Eurypylus' shield showed Heracles' sixth labor, which was to kill and chase away the Stymphalian birds. To escape wolves, they had migrated to a marsh in Arcadia. These birds killed human beings. Heracles could not go into the marsh because the soggy land would not support his weight, so Athena gave him some castanets. Heracles clicked the castanets, making noises that frightened the birds. He shot many of the birds, and the others flew away, never to return. Arcadia became much safer for mortals.

Eurypylus' shield showed Heracles' seventh labor, which was to capture the fire-breathing Cretan bull. This bull had been plaguing Crete, and King Minos wanted to be rid of it. Heracles choked the bull into submission and took it to Eurystheus, who released it. It wandered to Marathon and resumed its evil ways. Eurystheus lost an opportunity to help mortals when he released the dangerous bull instead of killing it. He should have sacrificed it to the gods.

Eurypylus' shield showed Heracles' eighth labor, which was to capture the man-eating mares of Diomedes of Thrace. Heracles took a few companions with him during this labor. He captured the horses, but they ate human flesh. While Heracles was fighting Diomedes, Heracles' companion Abderus watched the mares; unfortunately, they attacked and ate him. To avenge the death of Abderus, Heracles fed Diomedes to the mares. Heracles took the mares to Eurystheus, who ordered them to be taken to Mount Olympus and sacrificed to Zeus. Zeus did not want such a sacrifice, so he sent wild animals that killed the mares.

Eurypylus' shield showed Heracles' ninth labor, which was to get the war-belt of Hippolyta, the queen of the Amazons. The Amazons were war-like women who learned the skills of war such as archery from birth. Heracles sailed with other warriors to the Amazons, and Hippolyta met him. Heracles was in a hurry to get her war-belt, and he attempted to drag her by her hair from her horse. She respected Heracles' strength and daring, and she willingly gave him her war-belt. However, Hera caused trouble. She told the Amazons that Heracles was planning to kidnap Hippolyta, and the Amazons attacked Heracles, who sailed away with Hippolyta's war-belt. Penthesilea, Hippolyta's sister, later killed her with a spear in a hunting accident.

Eurypylus' shield showed Troy, which Heracles visited after he got the war-belt of Hippolyta. The gods Poseidon and Apollo had displeased Zeus, so he forced them to disguise themselves as mortals and work for Laomedon, King of Troy, for one year. Laomedon promised the two gods payment if they would build the walls of Troy; however, after the two gods had worked for a year and built the walls, Laomedon refused to give them the agreed-upon fee and even threatened to sell them into slavery. Poseidon and Apollo did not want to reveal themselves as gods because it would be humiliating if it became known that they had worked for a mortal, so they left. But Apollo sent a plague and Poseidon sent a sea-monster to Troy. Laomedon consulted seers, who told him that the plague would stop and the sea-monster would leave if he sacrificed Hesione, his daughter, to the sea-monster, so Laomedon chained Hesione by the sea. At this time, Heracles arrived and said that he would rescue Hesione if Laomedon would give him the valuable mares that Zeus had given to Laomedon when Zeus kidnapped Laomedon's son Ganymede and took him to Olympus to be his cupbearer. Heracles fought off the sea-monster with arrows and rescued Hesione, but Laomedon refused to give Heracles the mares that he had promised as payment. Heracles sailed away, but he promised to return later with more ships and conquer Troy. After he completed his twelve labors, he returned to Troy and conquered the city. He and his warriors killed all of Laomedon's sons except for Podarces, who saved his — Podarces' own — life by giving Heracles a golden veil that Hesione, Podarces' sister, had embroidered. Afterwards, Podarces used a new name that in his language is related to the word for "ransomed": Priam.

Eurypylus' shield showed Heracles' tenth labor, which was to steal the cattle of a monster named Geryon, who was three men joined together at the waist. Because of this, Geryon was called "triple-bodied Geryon." To get to Geryon's island, Heracles had to cross a desert. Heracles became so hot that he shot an arrow at Helios the Sun-god. Helios respected Heracles' daring, and he lent him a golden cup. Helios used the cup each night to sail from west to east on the ocean, and Heracles used it now to sail to the land of Geryon. Heracles was attacked there by a two-headed dog named Orthrus; the three-headed dog of Hades, Cerberus, was his brother. Heracles killed Orthrus with his club, and when Geryon's cowherd, Eurytion, attacked Heracles, Heracles also killed him with the club. Geryon then attacked Heracles, who shot and killed him with an arrow whose head had been dipped into the poisonous blood of the Hydra. Heracles put the cattle of Geryon into the golden cup of Helios, sailed back to the desert, and returned the golden cup to Helios. Heracles then took the cattle to Eurystheus.

Eurypylus' shield showed Heracles' eleventh labor, which was to steal some golden apples from the garden of the Hesperides. The shield also showed the fight between Heracles and Antaeus. Gaia, the goddess of the earth, had given the orchard that produced golden apples to Hera when Hera married Zeus. The Hesperides were nymphs who lived in the west and took care of the garden. To find out where the nymphs lived and how to get to them, Heracles captured the sea-god Nereus and held tightly to him as he changed into many shapes. Eventually, Nereus gave up and told Heracles the information he needed. On his way to the land of the Hesperides, Heracles met Antaeus, who challenged him to a wrestling match — the loser of the wrestling match would forfeit his life. Antaeus did this to collect the skulls of travelers so that when he had enough, he could build a temple out of them to Poseidon, his father. The mother of Antaeus was Gaia, the goddess of the earth. As long as Antaeus touched Gaia, he regained his strength. After throwing Antaeus to the earth a few times, Heracles discovered this secret, and he defeated Antaeus by holding him up in the air so that Antaeus' feet did not touch the earth and then strangling him. In the garden of the Hesperides, a dragon with a hundred heads guarded the golden apples, and Heracles fought and defeated the dragon. Heracles brought the golden apples to Eurystheus to show that he had completed the labor, and Athena then returned the golden apples to the Hesperides.

Eurypylus' shield showed Heracles' twelfth and final labor, which was to bring Cerberus, the three-headed guard dog of Hell, to Eurystheus. The shield also showed Heracles freeing Theseus from the Land of the Dead. Heracles visited Eleusis so that he could become initiated in the Eleusinian Mysteries and so learn how to go to and from the Land of the Dead while he was alive. Many entrances to the Land of the Dead exist, and Heracles used the one at Tanaerum. Heracles asked Hades for permission to take Cerberus to the Land of the Living, and Hades granted him permission as long as he did not use any weapons to subdue the three-headed dog. Using his bare hands and arms, Heracles subdued Cerberus and took him to Eurystheus to show that he had performed the final labor. Heracles then returned Cerberus to the Land of the Dead.

Eurypylus' shield showed Heracles' killing of the Centaur Nessus. Heracles had remarried. His new wife was Deianeira. One day, Heracles and Deianeira had to cross a river. Nessus offered to carry Deianeira across the river, but then he attempted to rape her. Heracles shot him with an arrow whose head had been dipped into the poisonous blood of the Hydra. Before Nessus died, he told Deianeira that his blood had a magical quality; it was a love potion. He said that if Deianeira were to ever think that Heracles was in love with someone else, she could make him love her again by smearing Nessus' blood on the inside of a robe and then giving it to Heracles to wear. Deianeira believed him, but it was a trick. She thought that Heracles was falling in love with someone else, so she did what Nessus had told her to do, but Heracles' arrow had poisoned the blood of the Centaur. When Heracles put on the robe, Nessus' blood, which was infected by the poisonous blood of the Hydra, burned Heracles like acid, as Nessus had known it would. In agony, Heracles climbed on a funeral pyre, lit it, and burned himself to death. Once dead, he became a god and lived on Mount Olympus.

The Trojans admired Eurypylus and his shield. Paris said to him, "Welcome. Now that you are here, I hope that we can kill the Greeks and set fire to their ships. I hope that your deeds will be like those of Heracles, your grandfather. You can keep Troy from being conquered."

Eurypylus replied, "Paris, the gods will decide who dies and who lives in the war. But I will fight for you and your city, and I promise you that I will not return to Troy until I have conquered the Greeks or the Greeks have killed me."

Eurypylus then chose Trojans to fight with him in the front lines: Paris, Aeneas, Polydamas, Pammon, Deiphobus, and Aethicus. All of these warriors were skilled at war. The Trojan warriors and their allies moved out to fight the Greeks; the Trojan warriors and their allies were like bees pouring out of a hive. The warriors and their horses made much noise as they went to fight the Greeks.

The Greeks also left their camps to fight in battle. The Trojans and the Greeks met and fought with rocks, swords, arrows, battleaxes, and spears. The blood of men and horses reddened the ground, and broken chariots mixed with broken bodies. Yet the warriors were eager to fight, as eager as calves kept near the herdsman's home are eager to be rejoined with their mothers when the cows return to the barn after grazing all day.

At first, the Greeks pushed back the Trojans, but then the Trojans gathered their strength and pushed back the Greeks. Eurypylus was mighty in battle. He killed Nireus, a Greek who was almost as handsome as Achilles but who had brought only three ships to Troy. Eurypylus speared Nireus a little above the waist, and Nireus fell. His blood gushed out of his body and soaked his armor and his hair. Nireus was like a young olive tree growing on the bank of a river that floods and tears away the bank and the young olive tree, which falls.

Eurypylus said, "Lie there, dead. You are a handsome man, but your good looks did not save your life. You met a much better man. In battle, strength is more important than beauty.

Eurypylus wanted to strip off Nireus' armor, but the Greek healer Machaon attacked him and tried to avenge the death of Nireus. Machaon speared Eurypylus in the right shoulder, and blood flowed out of the wound, but like a lion or boar that quickly strikes back at the hunter who has wounded it, Eurypylus speared Machaon in the groin. Despite his wound, Machaon lifted a rock and threw it at Eurypylus, whose helmet protected him. Eurypylus then thrust his spear into Machaon's chest and out his back. Machaon fell like a bull falls after a lion kills it.

Eurypylus said, "You are a fine healer, but not so fine a warrior. Your knowledge of medicine cannot help you now. Even your father, the skilled healer Asclepius, cannot help you now."

Machaon, because he was a dying man, had the gift of prophecy. He said, "Eurypylus, you do not have much longer to live. Your fate is coming quickly for you."

Machaon died, and Eurypylus said to the corpse, "Lie there, dead. As for my own death, I am not concerned about it. We mortals die; fate comes for us all."

Eurypylus then stabbed Machaon's corpse.

Teucer had been fighting elsewhere, but now he mourned because he saw that Eurypylus had killed both Machaon and Nireus. He called for help: "Greeks, help me to recover the corpses of Machaon and Nireus. It will be a disgrace to us if their corpses are carried away to Troy. We must recover their corpses and so win honor. Only by working hard in battle can we win honor."

The Greeks and the Trojans fought over the two corpses. Machaon's brother, Podalirius, had been healing wounded warriors by the ships, but when he learned that his brother had died, he put on armor and came to fight to recover his brother's corpse.

Podalirius killed Clitus, whose mother was a nymph. He also killed Lassus, whose mother was also a nymph: Pronoe. Pronoe gave birth to Lassus near a cave that is a holy place. Cold water flows through the cave, and in the rock of the cave appear what seem to be mixing bowls, nature-gods known as Pans, and nymphs. The cave had two entrances: one for mortal men, and one for immortal nymphs and gods. The entrance for mortals is difficult to use.

Many warriors died in the fight over the corpses of Machaon and Nireus, but the Greeks managed to recover their bodies and take them to their ships. But the Trojans and their allies — especially Eurypylus — began to attack fiercely and force back the Greeks. Little Ajax, Agamemnon, and Menelaus and a few other Greeks fought well and kept the Trojans and their allies from completely routing the Greeks.

Little Ajax speared Polydamas in the left shoulder but did not kill him. Polydamas retreated. Menelaus wounded Deiphobus in the right part of his chest, but did not kill him. Deiphobus also retreated. Agamemnon killed several of the enemy warriors and chased after Aethicus, who ran quickly and escaped death.

Eurypylus had driven many Greeks back to the ships. Now he attacked Little Ajax, Agamemnon, and Menelaus. Paris and Aeneas fought beside Eurypylus.

Aeneas threw a rock and hit Little Ajax, whose helmet saved his life. Little Ajax fell to the ground, but he was fated to die during his return to Greece, not during the Trojan War. Some of his fellow Greeks carried him back to the Greek ships.

Enemy warriors surrounded Agamemnon and Menelaus and tried to kill them. Agamemnon and Menelaus were like boars or lions that have been captured and put in an enclosure where they will fight armed men. Agamemnon and Menelaus killed warriors who came close to them. So many enemy warriors attacked them with arrows and rocks and spears that they would have died on that day, but Teucer, Idomeneus, Meriones, Thoas, and Thrasymedes came to help them. These five Greeks had run away from Eurypylus, but they faced him again to keep him from killing Agamemnon and Menelaus.

The Greek Teucer attacked Aeneas, but Aeneas' shield made of four oxhides stopped Teucer's spear. Still, Aeneas was forced to back up a short distance.

The Greek Meriones attacked Laophoon, who had come to Troy under the command of Asteropaeus. Meriones stabbed him under the naval and above his genitals, and when he pulled out his spear, he also pulled out Laophoon's intestines.

Alcimedes, a companion to Little Ajax, prayed to the gods and released a stone from his sling. It struck Hippasides, the charioteer of Pammon, on the temple. Hippasides fell from the chariot, and its wheels ran over him. Pammon mourned his death. A Trojan saved Pammon's life by coming to him and taking the reins.

Thrasymedes, the son of Nestor, wounded Acamas above a knee with a spear. Acamas retreated.

One of Eurypylus' companions speared the Greek Deiopites, one of Thoas' friends, in the chest. Deiopites tried to retreat, but Eurypylus ran after him and cut the tendons of his legs and killed him.

The Greek Thoas speared Paris in the right thigh. Paris retreated and got his bow and arrows from an aide so he could fight at a distance.

Idomeneus picked up a huge stone and threw it at Eurypylus, hitting his arm and causing him to drop his spear. The Greeks then forced Eurypylus back.

Because Eurypylus had dropped his spear, Agamemnon and Menelaus had a brief respite from battle, but Eurypylus' aides quickly brought him another spear, with which he killed many warriors.

Eurypylus fought so well that he made all the Greeks, including Agamemnon and Menelaus, retreat.

Eurypylus called to the Trojans and to his warriors, "The Greeks are running for their ships, just like sheep hurry to their enclosure at night. Let us kill as many Greeks as we can before night arrives."

The Trojans and their allies chased the Greeks just like dogs chase deer.

Eurypylus killed the Greeks Bucolion, Nesus, Chromius, and Antiphus, and many more warriors. To name all the warriors he killed would take much time.

Aeneas killed the Greeks Pheres and Antimachus, who had come to Troy from Crete under the command of Idomeneus.

Agenor killed the Greek Molus, who fell behind the other Greeks as they ran for the ships. Agenor's javelin hit Molus in the lower part of his right leg and shattered the bones. Molus' spirit went to the Land of the Dead.

Paris killed the Greeks Mosynus and Phorcys, two brothers who had come to Troy from the island of Salamis under the command of Great Ajax. Paris also killed Cleolaus, the aide of Meges. Paris' arrows were deadly. The arrow that killed Cleolaus lodged in his heart and quivered as long as the heart beat. Paris shot an arrow at Eetion and hit his jaw. Eetion screamed, and his tears mixed with blood.

For a large area of the battlefield, the only corpses were those of Greeks.

The Trojans and their allies could have burned the ships, but the arrival of night saved the Greeks. Eurypylus and the other Trojan allies and the Trojans camped by the Simois River and rejoiced in their victory. The Greeks mourned their many dead.

Chapter 7: Neoptolemus Comes to Troy

The next morning, many Greeks went out to meet the Trojans in battle, but some Greeks stayed in the camps so that they could bury Machaon and Nireus. The gods had blessed Nireus with beauty, but they had not blessed him with strength. The gods give gifts to mortals, but they do not give all their gifts to any one man. Still, the Greeks buried Nireus with full honors, just as they did Machaon. The Greeks built one funeral mound over their bones.

The battle continued, but Podalirius, the brother of Machaon, mourned his brother's death. Podalirius even thought of committing suicide with either a sword or a fatal drug. His friends spoke to him and attempted to comfort him, but Nestor said the words that meant the most.

Nestor told him, "Stop mourning like a woman mourning a fallen warrior. Mourning will not bring your brother back from death. He was born, and so death came to him. Endure your grief, just like I endure the grief I feel for the death of my son: Antilochus. My son was much like Machaon: skilled in war and of great intelligence. My son loved me. He died protecting me. Still, although I grieve, I eat, I stay alive, and I greet each new day, although I know that I am mortal and like everyone else I will die. Every man who has been born will someday die. While we are alive, we must accept what comes to us: both the good and the bad."

Podalirius replied, "I must mourn my brother: I owe him. He is the one who raised me after our father died and became a god. Although he was my brother, he treated me as if I were his son. He is the one who taught me how to properly use medicine. We ate at the same table and slept in the same bed, and we shared our possessions. I grieve so much that I no longer want to live."

Nestor said, "Every human being will mourn at sometime in their life. Every human being will someday die. We human beings do not all travel the same path while we are alive and we human beings do not always travel the path that we desire, but grief and death are things that all human beings have in common.

"Good fortunes and bad fortunes come from the gods, and the Fates mix them and without looking at where they land throw them down to earth, where they scatter as though a wind is blowing them. Sometimes a good man suffers misfortune that he does not deserve, and sometimes a bad man enjoys prosperity that he does not deserve. No man enjoys only good fortune his entire life. Because we live such a short time, we ought not to spend our time mourning. It is better to have hope: hope for better fortune.

"People say that we have an afterlife. The souls of good people go to a good place, and the souls of bad people go to a bad place. Your brother was a good man, and his father went to a good place. We can be sure that your brother went to a good place and joined his and your father."

Nestor raised Podalirius from the ground and walked with him to the ships. Podalirius still mourned, but he went with Nestor.

The battle continued, and Eurypylus killed many warriors, as did the Greeks. With his hands and feet splattered with blood that was not his own, Eurypylus killed Peneleus and other warriors. He was like his grandfather Heracles battling the Centaurs and killing them. A river can carve away its banks with swiftly flowing water and can batter and destroy dikes. Like that river, Eurypylus battered and destroyed Greeks.

Some Greeks saved their lives by running away. They rescued the body of Peneleus and carried it away to the ships, where they ran for protection from Eurypylus, to whom Heracles was giving great strength in battle. The Greeks stayed behind their defensive wall; they were like goats standing under an overhanging crag, using it for protection against snow and hail. The goats wait for the winter to end; the Greeks hoped that the attack of Eurypylus would end.

Athena gave the Greeks courage, and they kept Eurypylus from burning their ships. From their wall, the Greeks used arrows, rocks, and spears to repel the Trojans and their allies. The Greeks killed many warriors, and the defensive wall grew red with blood.

Eventually, the fighting came to a stop because the Greeks asked for a truce of two days so that both sides could bury their dead. Eurypylus agreed to the truce.

The Greeks mourned most the death of Peneleus and gave him a separate funeral pyre and burial mound. The other Greek corpses were burned at a distance in a common funeral pyre. The Trojans also burned their dead, and after the two-day truce, the fighting started again.

Odysseus and Diomedes made good time in their travel to the island of Scyros. When they arrived, Neoptolemus, Achilles' son, was practicing throwing spears and riding horses. Neoptolemus had heard of his father's death, and he mourned him, but he continued to practice the skills of war. Odysseus and Diomedes noticed Neoptolemus' strong resemblance to his father.

Neoptolemus greeted them, "Welcome. Please tell me who you are and where you are from and why you have come here."

Odysseus replied, "We are friends of your father, and we see the strong resemblance you have to your father. We are warriors you may have heard of. I am Odysseus, and my companion is Diomedes. We have come to you and to your mother, Deidamia, because we want you to come to Troy and fight for us. A prophecy says that we will win the war if you fight for us. If you do, you will receive many gifts from the Greeks. I will give you the armor that Hephaestus made for your father; the armor is a work of art. The only person who has used this armor is your father, whom all Greek warriors and I respected. When your father died, I brought his corpse back to our ships, and I killed many Trojans as I defended your father's corpse. Because of these actions, Thetis gave me the armor."

Diomedes thought, *Odysseus is taking sole credit for a group effort. Certainly, Great Ajax was instrumental in protecting the corpse of Achilles. Many other Greeks also helped in that effort.*

Odysseus continued, "After you come to the war, I will gladly give you your father's armor. And after the war is over, Menelaus will become your father-in-law: He wants you to marry his daughter, Hermione. He will also give you gold and other gifts."

Neoptolemus replied, "The prophecies will come true. Tomorrow, let us set sail for Troy. Tonight, let us go into the palace so that I may entertain you."

They entered the palace and saw Deidamia, who was thin because she was mourning the death of her husband, Achilles. She would mourn more when she learned that her son, Neoptolemus, was going to Troy. Neoptolemus told her the names of Odysseus and Diomedes, but he resolved not to tell her until the morning that he was going to Troy so that she would not grieve that night and so that she would not spend the night trying to persuade him not to go. All ate, and then most slept.

Deidamia did not sleep. Odysseus and Diomedes had persuaded her husband, Achilles, to go to war. He had died and made her a widow, and she was afraid that Odysseus and Diomedes would convince her son to go to war.

At dawn, Neoptolemus told her that he was sailing to Troy with Odysseus and Diomedes. She screamed and held on to her son, wrapping her arms around him and begging him not to go. She cried as loudly as does a cow searching for a lost calf.

Deidamia said to her son, "Why are you going to Troy? Many men — experienced and skillful warriors — have died there. You are very young and totally inexperienced in war. Stay here so that the day will not come when I learn that you have died at Troy like your father. These men persuaded your father to go to Troy, and now they are trying to persuade you to go to Troy. If your father, as strong and as skilled as he was, and who had a goddess for his mother, died at Troy, do you think that you will return from Troy alive? If you die, I will be wretched. The worst pain a woman can feel comes from knowing that her husband and her son have died and she has no one to protect her. Men do not respect a widow without a son; they take away her land and possessions. They ignore justice."

Neoptolemus replied, "No man can go against his fate. If I am fated to die at Troy, then I will die there. If I do die there, I hope that I shall accomplish great deeds before I die."

Neoptolemus' maternal grandfather, Lycomedes, said to him, "You are brave and strong like your father, but what you are doing is dangerous. Not only is fighting in battle dangerous, but sailing over the sea in ships is dangerous. Sailing both to and from Troy will be dangerous; many sailors do not return to port."

Lycomedes kissed Neoptolemus and said no more to dissuade him from going to Troy. Deidamia, however, kept talking to him and trying to convince him to remain at home. Neoptolemus, however, was eager to leave. While Deidamia delayed him with talk, Neoptolemus was restless like a horse eager to compete in a race; the horse's feet dance continually because it is eager to start the race. Deidamia was proud of her son's spirit, although she worried about his safety.

Neoptolemus kissed his mother many times and then left the palace. She stayed behind, grieving. She was like a swallow that mourns the nestlings that a snake has eaten. The swallow flits here and there, crying out in grief. Deidamia wandered through her son's room, crying on his bed or handling each of his possessions and kissing it, whether the possession were a child's toy or a man's weapon.

Neoptolemus went to the ship with Odysseus and Diomedes and twenty men whom Deidamia had sent to be her son's aides. Thetis, the Nereids, and Poseidon looked at Neoptolemus and rejoiced. He was brave and strong and eager to go to Troy. In battle, he would look like Ares, scowling in anger and fighting fiercely, although he was young and still without a beard. The townspeople on the island of Scyros prayed for Neoptolemus to return safely, and the gods heard their prayers: Neoptolemus would not die at Troy.

They set sail, and Poseidon made the sailing safe because he wanted the ship to quickly arrive at Troy, where Eurypylus and the Trojans were harrying the Greeks. Odysseus and Diomedes sat by Neoptolemus and told him stories about Troy and his father's heroic deeds in battles both by land and by sea, both in the land of Telephus and at Troy. Neoptolemus longed to win fame in war.

From the palace, Deidamia mourned as the ship sailed away. Mothers worry about sons, even when the sons simply eat an evening meal elsewhere. Deidamia continued to mourn after she could no longer see the ship's sails.

The ship sailed all day and all night and sailed past the burial mound of Achilles. Odysseus did not tell Neoptolemus when they passed his father's burial mound because he did not want him to mourn. The ship also passed the burial mound of Protesilaus, the first Greek to be killed in the Trojan War. Above his burial mound rise tall trees, the tops of which wither when they are high enough to be within sight of Troy. When the ship reached the Greek camp, the Greeks were busy fighting the Trojans at the defensive wall, which Eurypylus was trying to knock down. The Greeks were weaker with Odysseus and Diomedes absent and not fighting for them.

Diomedes said to the warriors on the ship, "We need to put on our armor and go to the battle at once, or the Trojans will knock down our wall and burn our ships. If that happens, we will die at Troy and never return home and see our wives and children."

The ship had landed closest to the camp of Odysseus, so to save time everyone went there and put on armor that Odysseus and his men had stripped from warriors whom they had killed. The best warriors put on the best armor, as was fitting.

Diomedes put on the excellent armor that Odysseus had stripped from the Trojan Socus. Neoptolemus was eager to fight, just like his father had been. Neoptolemus put on his father's armor, which fit him, due to the skill of Hephaestus. The gods made Neoptolemus strong enough that he could use his father's spear.

The Greeks who saw Neoptolemus arrive at the battle wanted to welcome him, but because of the heavy fighting, they could not. They felt like sailors who have been forced to stay on a desert island for a long time because the winds are blowing in the wrong direction. They are running out of food when favorable winds come and they can sail to civilization. The Greeks had longed for help, and they got it.

Neoptolemus was like a lion that sees hunters approaching its cave, eager to drag away the lion's cubs. The lion roars and races to the cave, eager to protect its cubs and to kill the hunters. Neoptolemus was eager to go to war, and he went to where the battle was being most fiercely fought: the place where the defensive wall of the Greek camp was weakest.

Eurypylus and other enemy warriors were trying to destroy a tower, but Neoptolemus, Odysseus, Diomedes, Leonteus, and the other Greeks forced them back. The Greeks were like herdsmen and dogs chasing lions away from the herdsmen's cattle; the lions are fierce and hungry, but they are forced to back away from the herd — a short distance.

Eurypylus encouraged his warriors to keep fighting so that they could burn the Greeks' ships. He picked up a huge rock and hurled it at the defensive wall. The foundations of the wall cracked, but the Greeks kept fighting. They were like jackals or wolves that hunters are trying to drive out of a cave and away from their pups so that the hunters can kill the pups. The jackals or wolves stand firm, challenging the hunters and their weapons.

Eurypylus yelled at the Greeks, "You are cowards. The only reason you are not dead yet is because of your defensive wall, which protects you. You are like dogs that are afraid to fight a lion; that is why you stay behind your wall. Fight out on the plain; meet me face to face, and I will kill you."

So he yelled, but this would not happen. His fate was coming to him: Neoptolemus would soon spear him and take away his life.

Neoptolemus fought from the Greeks' wall and killed many enemy warriors. The Trojans retreated, and they crowded around Eurypylus the way that children crowd around their father's knees when Zeus' lightning frightens them.

Neoptolemus frightened the Trojans, who saw that he was wearing Achilles' armor and who thought that Achilles had come back to the Land of the Living. The Trojans did not tell Eurypylus that they thought that Achilles was fighting again; they did not want to frighten Eurypylus and his warriors.

The Trojans were like men who see a dangerous torrent of water across their path. The men must cross the water to continue their journey although they prefer not to. They stand and look at the raging water. The Trojans stayed by the Greeks' defensive wall although they wanted to flee.

Eurypylus continued to encourage the Trojans to fight. He believed that Neoptolemus would grow tired because he had killed so many warriors in the battle, but Neoptolemus did not grow tired.

Athena watched the battle from Mount Olympus. She flew from Mount Olympus to a hill close to Troy and gave the Greeks strength and courage in battle.

Neoptolemus continued to kill. Zeus was one of his ancestors, and Neoptolemus had the strength of his father, Achilles. He was like a fisherman spearing fish. The fisherman fishes at night, and when fish come close to the ship because they see the gleam of fire, the fisherman spears them with a trident. Neoptolemus speared Trojans when they came close to the wall.

All the warriors on both sides fought hard, and almost all the warriors grew tired, but Neoptolemus stayed strong and unafraid. He was as unwearied as a river. He was as brave as a river that does not feel fear even as a forest fire burns closer to it. The river has nothing to fear because when fire touches water, the fire goes out.

The Trojans threw spears at Neoptolemus, but none inflicted a wound: The armor of his father protected him. Neoptolemus encouraged the Greeks to fight, and he wanted to kill many Trojans because his father had died at Troy.

Neoptolemus killed Celtus and Eubius, the twin sons of Meges, who was wealthy. Celtus and Eubius were born on the same day, and they died on the same day after a short life. Neoptolemus killed one with a javelin that entered his heart and the other with a rock that crushed his helmet and his brain. Many other warriors died, too.

Evening arrived, and the two armies separated. Neoptolemus, Odysseus, and Diomedes had arrived in time to defend the walls and to keep Eurypylus and the Trojans from burning the Greek ships. The battle ended for this day.

Phoenix came to Neoptolemus and marveled at how much he resembled his father, Achilles. Phoenix felt joy when he looked at Neoptolemus, and he felt sadness when he remembered Achilles. Despite the happiness that Phoenix felt, he cried.

Phoenix hugged Neoptolemus and said to him, "Welcome. I took care of your father when he was little. I treated him like my son, and he treated me like his father. He had great strength and courage, and so do you. I mourn him, and I wish that I had died before he did, but I don't want you to be sad. Instead, concentrate on fighting, and especially on fighting Eurypylus. You are a better warrior than he is, just as your father, Achilles, was a better warrior than Eurypylus' father, Telephus, and you will win glory if you fight him."

Neoptolemus said, "Fate and Ares will witness me and Eurypylus in battle, and Fate and Ares will pass judgment on our fighting ability."

Neoptolemus wanted to go past the Greeks' defensive wall and fight Eurypylus immediately, but night made that impossible.

The Greeks were happy as they praised Neoptolemus. Many Greeks gave him gifts: gold, silver, slave-women, bronze, iron, red wine, horses, armor, and clothing. Neoptolemus rejoiced.

Agamemnon said to him, "You are definitely the son of Achilles. You have your father's strength, beauty, size, and courage. With your help, we shall defeat Troy. When I look at you, I remember the time that your father, with his head blazing with non-burning fire sent by Athena, shouted at the Trojans, panicking them and helping the Greeks bring the corpse of Patroclus to our ships. Your father is now a god, and I feel that he sent you to us."

Neoptolemus replied, "I wish that my father were still alive so that he could see me fight. I do not think that he would be ashamed of me."

After eating, Neoptolemus went to his father's camp and looked at the armor of warriors whom his father had killed. Achilles' slave-women were attending to their tasks. Neoptolemus mourned for his father. After hunters kill a lion, the lion's cub goes into its lair and sees the bones of animals its parent has killed. The cub mourns the death of its parent. Just like that, Neoptolemus mourned the death of Achilles.

The slave-women admired Neoptolemus, and Briseis looked at him and rejoiced at seeing him but also mourned for Achilles.

The Trojans paid respect to Eurypylus in their camps, just as the Greeks paid respect to Neoptolemus in their camps. Then everyone except the guards slept.

Chapter 8: The Death of Eurypylus

At dawn, both armies prepared for battle. Neoptolemus urged the Greeks to fight well, and Eurypylus urged the Trojans and their allies to fight well. On this day, Eurypylus wanted to destroy the Greeks' defensive wall and burn their ships and destroy their army. The Fates knew what Eurypylus wanted to do, and they laughed.

Neoptolemus said to the Myrmidons, his father's warriors, "We need to be the saviors of the Greeks and a disaster to the Trojans. Let us be courageous and without fear — fear takes away strength and courage in battle. Let us fight so well that the Trojans will think that Achilles has returned to the Land of the Living and is fighting again."

Neoptolemus put on his father's armor; Thetis was proud of him. Automedon, his charioteer, then drove Neoptolemus' father's horses into battle. The horses were happy that Neoptolemus so resembled his father: Both men were heroes. The morale of the Greeks was high as Neoptolemus led them into battle — the Greek warriors were like wasps that have been disturbed and pour out of their nest to attack.

The plain in front of Troy filled with the two armies. They charged and fought, and dust rose high on the plain and the air filled with the noise of battle. The battle was like a storm at sea, and it was like two storms crashing against each other in the sky when Zeus is angry that mortals do not honor Themis, the goddess of justice. Eris, the goddess of strife, was happy as she witnessed the battle.

Neoptolemus killed the brothers Melaneus and Alcidamas, sons of Alexinomus. He also killed Menes, Morys, Polybus, Hippomedon, and other enemy warriors. He covered the ground with the corpses of Trojans and their allies, and he destroyed the Trojans the way that a wind-blown fire destroys dry brush.

But the Trojans continued to fight. Aeneas killed Aristolochus, splintering his helmet and his skull with a rock.

Diomedes killed Eumaeus, who lived on a mountain in Dardania, the mountain where Anchises had lived and where he had slept with the goddess Aphrodite, who gave birth to Aeneas.

Agamemnon killed Stratus, who had come to Troy from Thrace.

The Greek Meriones killed Chlemus, who had become a king when Glaucus died.

Eurypylus also killed many warriors. He killed Eurytus, Menoetius, and Harpalus. Harpalus was one of Odysseus' friends, but Odysseus was fighting in another part of the battlefield and could not prevent his death or protect his corpse. The Greek Antiphus, one of Harpalus' friends, threw a spear at Euryalus but missed and killed Meilanion.

Eurypylus was angry at the death of Meilanion and rushed at Antiphus, who fled and escaped his death for now. He was not fated to die at Troy; later, when Antiphus tried to sail home with Odysseus to Ithaca, Antiphus would be the last Greek whom the Cyclops Polyphemus would eat before Odysseus and the other surviving Greeks blinded him.

Eurypylus killed many Greeks. Their corpses lay on the ground, as do tall trees that have been felled by woodsmen.

Eurypylus and Neoptolemus met on the battlefield. Eurypylus asked Neoptolemus, "Who are you, and whose horses do you have? Why are you fighting here against me, who will soon kill you? All who have fought me have died, and dogs have feasted on their flesh and left only the bones."

Neoptolemus replied, "Why are you asking me questions as if I were one of your friends? But let me answer them. I am the son of Achilles, who injured your father, Telephus, and then cured the wound. These horses, which can run even over the sea, belonged to my father. This spear also belonged to my father; its wood came from Mount Pelion."

Neoptolemus jumped from his chariot to the ground, and Eurypylus lifted a heavy rock and threw it, but Neoptolemus' shield protected him. Neoptolemus was like a crag that a swiftly flowing river tries to batter but the river cannot move it.

The two warriors rushed at each other like hungry wild animals that fight over an ox or stag that one of them has killed. Other warriors also fought in the front lines of battle.

Eurypylus and Neoptolemus attacked and tried to kill each other; they made Eris happy. Sweat streamed from the two warriors as their weapons clanged on each other's shields.

The gods watched from Mount Olympus as the two warriors fought. Some gods supported Eurypylus, and some gods supported Neoptolemus. Finally, Neoptolemus speared Eurypylus through the throat, and his blood gushed out along with his spirit as darkness overcame him. As his blood gushed out, his body grew pale.

Neoptolemus said, "Eurypylus, you must have thought that you would defeat the Greeks and burn their ships and kill all of us here at Troy. The gods did not allow that to happen. Instead, my father's spear has killed you, as it will kill any mortal man who fights me. Even if the man were made of bronze, my father's spear would kill him."

The Trojans were terrified as Neoptolemus stripped off the armor of Eurypylus and gave it to his aides to take back to his camp by his ships. Neoptolemus mounted his chariot and charged against the Trojans as if he were a thunderbolt that all except Zeus fears as it shatters trees and rocks. Neoptolemus killed many Trojans. Their corpses covered the ground and made it red just as leaves in autumn turn red and fall and make the ground red.

Neoptolemus and the Greeks would have forced the Trojans to run inside the walls of Troy the way that lions force cattle to run to their stalls or the way that a storm forces pigs to run for shelter, but Ares — without the knowledge of the other gods — came down from Mount Olympus to help the Trojans prevent a rout. His four fire-breathing horses — Aethon, Conabus, Phlogius, and Phobus — pulled his chariot. The horses' parents were a Fury and the god of the North wind. Ares called to the Trojans to stay and fight the Greeks. The Trojans heard his voice but did not see him or his horses — Ares was hidden in a mist.

The prophet Helenus, one of Hector's brothers, heard Ares and shouted to the Trojans, "Don't retreat! Stay and fight! Neoptolemus is only a mortal, like his late father. We have the immortal Ares, god of war, helping us. Ares orders us to fight the Greeks — now! Be bold! Be courageous! We have a mighty god on our side."

The Trojans listened to Helenus and faced the Greeks and fought them, the way that dogs that have run from a wolf that wants to eat the sheep the dogs are supposed to defend turn around and fight the wolf when they hear the shepherd shouting orders at them.

The two armies fought, and men died, and the two armies were equal in strength and courage. Imagine workers going down two lines of vines in a vineyard and trimming them. The pieces they trim fall to the ground. Just like that, dead warriors from both armies fell to the ground. Equal numbers of warriors on both sides fell. The Trojans fought well because Ares was on their side; the Greeks fought well because Neoptolemus was on their side. Blood splattered the warriors on both sides, and it splattered Ares and Enyo, the god and goddess of war. Enyo enjoyed the equal slaughter by evenly matched armies. Not wanting to anger either Thetis or Ares, she did not help either army.

Neoptolemus killed Perimedes, Cestrus, Phaleris, Perilaus, and Menalces, the only son of Medon, a skilled craftsman. After Medon died, distant relatives divided his possessions among themselves.

The Trojan Deiphobus killed Lycon with a spear a little above the groin. Lycon's intestines poured out through the wound caused by Deiphobus' spear.

Aeneas killed Dymas, who came from Aulis but never again returned home.

The Greek Euryalus killed Astraeus with a spear to the stomach. Food mixed with blood exited the wound.

The Trojan Agenor killed Hippomenes, one of Teucer's friends.

Angry at the death of his friend, Teucer shot an arrow at Agenor, but he missed and hit Deiophontes. The Fates, who send weapons wherever they want, sent the arrow through his left eye to his right ear. Deiophontes jumped, and Teucer shot an arrow at his throat and cut the tendons in his neck and killed him.

The work of war is killing men, and warriors on both sides did their work well. Eris and Ares gloried in the slaughter, and the Fates did not rest.

Ares gave the Trojans courage and he sent fear to the Greeks, but Neoptolemus remained unafraid. He killed Trojans as easily as a boy kills flies that swarm around a pail of milk. The boy is proud of his kills, and so was Neoptolemus, who was like a mountain crag standing firm as winds blast it.

Ares became angry at Neoptolemus, who was killing Trojans whom Ares respected, and Ares would have fought him, but Athena came down to Mount Ida. She carried her aegis, the shield on which were depicted fire-breathing dragons, and she wore her helmet and armor from which lightning flashed. The earth shook. She would have fought Ares, but Zeus sent thunder to warn the two immortals to withdraw from the war that mortals were fighting. Ares departed for Thrace, and Athena departed for Athens.

Now the Trojans, exhausted from fighting, retreated to Troy, pursued by Greeks. Just like dogs chasing deer, the Greeks chased Trojans. Neoptolemus killed many Trojans as they fled.

Routed, the Trojans withdrew behind the walls of Troy. The Greeks rested from killing Trojans, just as oxen rest after having pulled the plow and labored long. After a brief respite from fighting, the Greeks circled Troy and prepared to attack. Inside the city, the Trojans made sure their gates were tightly secured. They were like shepherds in a sheepfold who are preparing for a storm that they know is coming. The Greeks made much noise as they came toward the city. They were like hungry jawdaws or starlings that cry loudly as they eat olives hanging from olive trees.

The battle started again as the Greeks attacked the gates and the Trojans defended the gates with arrows, rocks, and spears.

The Greek Meriones shot an arrow that hit Phylodamas under the jaw and in the throat. Polites, a son of Priam, was one of Phylodamas' friends. Phylodamas fell from the tower like a vulture that has been sitting on a crag falls after an arrow hits the vulture.

Meriones shot another arrow, hoping to kill Polites, who swerved out of the way of the arrow and saved his life just like a sailor who sees a dangerous rock in the sea moves the ship's rudder and avoids death.

Warriors on both sides bled and died, and the blood of Trojans streamed down the walls of Troy. The Greeks were the superior fighting force and would have conquered Troy on this day except that Ganymede, the cupbearer of Zeus, made an appeal to the father of gods and men: "Zeus, hear me. I am one of your descendants, and although I was mortal, I now live as an immortal among the gods on Mount Olympus. I am in pain as I see the agonies that Troy is undergoing. I do not want to see the city fall, and I do not want to see its citizens die. Please take that sight away from me."

Zeus saved the city; it was not fated to fall on this day. The god sent fog that covered the city, and no Greek could see its walls. Lightning flashed, and thunder rumbled.

Nestor shouted to the Greeks, "Zeus is sending a message to us. We must no longer attack Troy on this day. We must stop fighting and return to our ships. No mortal should oppose the will of Zeus: He is too powerful. When the Titans attacked him, he burned the land and he boiled the sea. He dried up the streams and rivers, and he destroyed many living things. He filled the sky with fire.

"Let us return to the ships now. On another day, Zeus will favor us the way that he now favors the Trojans. Calchas told us that Troy would fall in the tenth year of the war, but it will not fall today."

The Greeks knew that Nestor was a good advisor, and they obeyed him. They collected their dead from the battlefield and gave the corpses a proper burial — the battlefield was clear of fog. Then the Greeks returned to their ships and washed away their sweat and blood.

Night arrived, and the Greeks honored Neoptolemus, who was not tired because his grandmother Thetis took away all the pains that follow fierce fighting.

After the evening meal, the Greeks and the Trojans set guards and then slept. The Greeks were afraid that the Trojans might attack, and the Trojans were afraid that the Greeks might attack.

Chapter 9: The Return of Philoctetes

By dawn, the fog that Zeus had sent to hide the walls of Troy had dissipated. The Greeks looked at the city — it seemed as if it had never been hidden by fog. The Trojans stayed in the city. They were afraid to fight the Greeks; they believed that Achilles might still be alive and fighting.

The Trojan Antenor prayed to Zeus, "Stop this warrior who is killing so many of us, whoever he is. He may be Achilles, whom we thought to be in the Land of the Dead, or he may be another great warrior. Zeus, please help us — do not help the Greeks. Many Trojans are dying now. You must have forgotten that your own son Dardanus is one of our ancestors. If you want Trojans to die and Troy to fall, please bring that about quickly. We prefer that to our having to suffer for a long time."

Zeus heard the prayer. Soon many Trojans would die and Troy would fall; Zeus would not keep Neoptolemus from killing Trojans. Instead, Zeus gave Neoptolemus strength and courage because he wanted Thetis to be proud of her grandson.

Priam sent Menoetes, a herald, to Agamemnon to ask for a temporary truce, which Agamemnon readily granted. Anger ought not to be directed toward the dead. The Greeks and the Trojans held funerals; they burned many dead warriors on funeral pyres. They also burned many dead horses.

The Trojans especially honored Eurypylus; they buried him in front of the Dardanian Gate, apart from other warriors.

Neoptolemus visited his father's tomb to mourn. He kissed the memorial pillar and then said, "Father, hello. I will never forget you. I wish that you had still been living when I came to the war at Troy. We could have known each other, we could have fought the Trojans together, and perhaps we could have taken much treasure home. Those things did not happen. But the Trojans feared you, and now they fear me. You fought well for the Greeks, and now I am fighting well for the Greeks."

Neoptolemus, Phoenix, and twelve other Myrmidons mourned at the tomb of Achilles, and then they returned to their camp and slept through the night.

At dawn, the Greeks ate and then armed for battle and marched to the walls of Troy. Dust rose into the air, and the warriors shouted. Trojans heard the shout, and almost all felt despair.

The Trojan Deiphobus felt bold and fearless. He said to the Trojans, "Remember what we are fighting for. We are not fighting just for Paris and Helen. We are fighting for Troy and for our wives and our children and our aged parents. I prefer fighting and dying in battle to seeing my city conquered. Do not be afraid. Do not think that Achilles is fighting you — we know that the Greeks burned his corpse and so his spirit is in the Land of the Dead. Because we are defending our city, we ought to be willing to fight whatever warrior has replaced Achilles. We have suffered much in battle, but let us continue to fight. Food and wealth follow hard work. Spring follows winter. Health returns after an illness. Peace follows war. With time, all things change."

The Trojans armed for battle. Here, a weeping wife, afraid for her husband, brought him his armor. There, small children brought their father pieces of his armor. The father knew that the children worried about him, but he smiled proudly at them. In another place, an aged father helped his son put on protective armor and urged him to fight fiercely and showed him scars — mementos — on his chest from the time when the aged father was a warrior. The Trojan warriors knew the fear and pain their relatives felt, but the warriors were eager to defend their families and their city.

The Trojans warriors left their city, and the battle started. Cavalry fought other cavalry, infantry fought other infantry, and warriors in chariots fought other warriors in chariots. Both sides shouted. Arrows and spears sped through the air. Weapons clanged against shields. Battle-axes killed warriors, and armor turned red with blood.

The Trojan women — wives, mothers, daughters, and sisters — watched from the walls and prayed for husbands and sons and fathers and brothers. The old men of Troy watched with them. Only Helen, ashamed that so many warriors were dying because of her, stayed in her quarters with her female servants.

The Trojan Deiphobus killed a charioteer, Hippasides, who fell from the chariot. Hippasides' comrade-in-arms with whom Hippasides went to war in the same chariot was afraid that Deiphobus would now kill him, but

Melanthius climbed onto the chariot, seized the reins, and drove him to safety. Melanthius had no whip, so he used his spear to hit the horses.

Deiphobus killed many Greeks. They fell the way that trees fall when a tree cutter fells a forest in order to make charcoal. Many Greeks fled to the Scamander River, and Deiphobus followed them and continued to kill. Fishermen sometimes drag a net filled with swordfish into shallow water, and a fisherman goes into the water and kills the swordfish with a weapon and the water turns red with their blood. Just like that, Deiphobus went into the river after the fleeing Greeks, killed them, and turned the water red with their blood.

In another part of the battle, Neoptolemus was killing many Trojans. Thetis felt proud of her grandson just as she had previously felt proud of her son. As she watched Neoptolemus in battle, she remembered Achilles and mourned for him. Neoptolemus killed Amides, who was on horseback. Neoptolemus' spear hit Amides in the stomach, and the point of the spear hit his spine. Amides' intestines came out through the wound. Neoptolemus also killed Ascanius and Oenops with his spear, wounding one in the mouth and the other in the throat. Neoptolemus killed many men, yet he did not grow tired. Warriors fell before Neoptolemus the way that olives fall before a harvester who hits them with a stick.

In another part of the battlefield, Diomedes, Agamemnon, and other Greeks were fighting. Many Trojans bravely fought them, but others were afraid and fled from the Greeks.

Neoptolemus became aware that many Greeks were being slaughtered at the Scamander River, so he ordered his charioteer, Automedon, to drive him to the river so he could fight there. As they approached the Trojans, Neoptolemus resembled Ares.

Automedon recognized Deiphobus, and he said to Neoptolemus, "This is one of the sons of Priam and Hecuba: Deiphobus. When your father was alive, Deiphobus was afraid to fight him. Now some god has made Deiphobus brave."

Neoptolemus urged Automedon to drive the chariot faster. Deiphobus saw Neoptolemus approaching, and he was not sure what to do: flee or fight. A boar can chase jackals away from its young and then see a fierce lion. The boar does not know what to do: It is afraid to fight the fierce lion, but it wants to protect its young. Deiphobus was afraid to fight Neoptolemus, but he wanted to protect his city. Neoptolemus shouted to Deiphobus, "You are killing Greeks who are not great warriors! If you think that you are a great warrior, then fight me!"

With Automedon driving the chariot, Neoptolemus charged upon Deiphobus and would have killed him if Apollo had not filled the air with fog and grabbed Deiphobus and taken him safely away to Troy, where many Trojans were fleeing for safety. Neoptolemus' spear that would have stabbed Deiphobus stabbed only air.

Disappointed, Neoptolemus said, "You have escaped me, but not because of anything that you did. A god has saved you from me."

Zeus dissipated the fog, and Neoptolemus saw the Trojans fleeing to Troy. Neoptolemus charged toward the Trojans, who were afraid the way that sailors are afraid when they see a huge wave rushing toward their ship.

Neoptolemus yelled to the Greeks, "Be brave, and be bold. We are on the verge of victory. We Greeks have been at Troy far too long. It is time that we conquered the city. We should not be weak like women. It is better to be dead than to be thought to be weak and unwarlike."

The Greeks attacked the Trojans, and both sides fought bravely. The Greeks fought to conquer the city; the Trojans fought to keep their city from being conquered.

Apollo wanted to help the Trojans, so he came down from Mount Olympus and landed by the Xanthus River. Apollo shouted, and the Greeks felt afraid while the Trojans felt brave. Poseidon reacted by making the Greeks brave, and both sides fought bravely.

Angry, Apollo wanted to kill Neoptolemus in the same way that he had killed Achilles: He wanted to shoot an arrow into Neoptolemus' ankle. But birds of omen shrieked on his left — the unlucky side. Neoptolemus was not fated to die on this day.

Apollo was tempted to disregard the bad omens and kill Neoptolemus, but Poseidon came to him and said, "Stop! Zeus will be angry if you kill Neoptolemus. The death of the son of Achilles will make the other immortals of the sea and me unhappy, the way we were when Achilles died. Leave now, without killing Neoptolemus. If you stay here, I will open a wide crack in the earth and push Troy into it and then close the crack again so that Troy will be forever under ground and in darkness. You do not want that to happen."

Apollo departed from the battlefield, and then Poseidon departed. The two armies continued to fight until the prophet Calchas advised the Greeks to withdraw to the ships because he had learned through divination that Troy would not fall until Philoctetes rejoined the Greeks.

Philoctetes had been with the Greeks at the start of the war. He had sailed with their ships from Aulis but had never reached Troy. When the Greeks camped on an island during the voyage, a poisonous water-snake had bitten Philoctetes and he had never recovered from the wound, which festered and stank and caused him to cry out because of the pain. The Greeks had abandoned him on the island of Lemnos and had sailed to Troy. For ten years, Philoctetes had lived alone in a cave on the island. A master archer, he killed enough birds to stay alive.

Following the advice of Calchas, Agamemnon and Menelaus sent Odysseus and Diomedes to Lemnos to find and bring back Philoctetes.

Odysseus and Diomedes arrived at the city of Hephaestus on Lemnos; this city was known for great wrong. The women of the city had exacted a terrible vengeance on their husbands, who were ignoring them and instead sleeping with slave-women whom they had gotten when they fought a war against Thrace. Filled with jealousy, the women had killed their husbands all on the same night. Philoctetes would likely want to kill Odysseus and Diomedes because the Greeks had abandoned him on the island ten years previously.

Odysseus and Diomedes found the cave where Philoctetes had taken refuge. Philoctetes was lying on the ground and groaning because of pain. The feathers of many birds lay on the floor of the cave. Philoctetes had shot the birds with his arrows so he could eat them and sew together some of their feathers to make a blanket. He tried to treat his wound, but he was unable to stop the pain for very long.

Philoctetes had long hair that resembled that of a wild beast whose paw is caught in a trap. The wild beast gnaws off its paw so that it can escape from the trap and return to its lair, where it suffers from hunger and pain. Philoctetes was like that wild beast. He was very thin, and he was very dirty. He and his wound stank. Exhausted by pain, he lay on the floor of the cave, and his eyes were sunk deeply into their sockets.

Philoctetes kept groaning because of pain. His wound, which was in his foot, was black and infected. The sea can cut away a crag by pounding and destroying its base over time. Philoctetes' life was being cut away by his wound, which slowly grew worse over time. Pus dripped from the wound onto the floor of the cave. By Philoctetes was his quiver filled with arrows and his bow, which Heracles had made and given to him. Philoctetes had dipped the heads of some of the arrows in the deadly poison of the water-snake; Philoctetes used these arrows against enemies. The other arrows were for hunting.

Philoctetes saw Odysseus and Diomedes, and his first thought was to kill them with his poisoned arrows. He grabbed his bow and arrows, but through the agency of Athena, he quickly decided not to kill them.

Sorrowing, Odysseus and Diomedes came to him and spoke to him. They asked about his wound, and they said that the Greeks had a skilled doctor who had learned much by treating wounds and injuries during the war and who could cure him if he returned to the Greeks. They also told him that a prophecy had said that Troy would fall if he fought for the Greeks. In addition, they asked him not to blame the Greeks for his ills, but to blame the Fates: "They are the ones who bring all ills and all goods to mortals. They can bring good things to a man who has suffered evil things, and they can bring evil things to a man who has enjoyed good things. They wander the world, and no one can escape them." Philoctetes listened, and he agreed to go to Troy.

Odysseus and Diomedes carried him to their ship, and they washed his wound with sponges and lots of water — this lessened the pain, a little. They prepared a good meal for him, which he greatly enjoyed. At dawn, they set sail for Troy, and dolphins swam beside their ship. Athena sent them a favorable wind.

The Greeks were happy to see Philoctetes, who held on to Odysseus and Diomedes and limped into the camp. A woodcutter can cut halfway through the trunk of a pine tree in order to make a torch of its resinous wood. The tree is weakened and leans against saplings that support its weight. Philoctetes was like that pine tree.

The Greeks saw Philoctetes' wound and pitied him, and then Podalirius, son of the famous physician Asclepius, demonstrated his skill in healing. He applied drugs to the wound and prayed to his father for help, and the Greeks washed Philoctetes and rubbed him with olive oil. His pain disappeared, and color came into his face. He gained weight, and the Greeks rejoiced. A grain field looks bleak during the winter, but with the arrival of spring it begins to flourish. Philoctetes began to flourish.

Soon, Philoctetes' wound had healed, and Athena had made him the man he was before the poisonous snake had bitten him. In his honor, Agamemnon held a banquet. After Philoctetes and the other Greeks had eaten their fill, Agamemnon said to him, "Please do not be angry at us because we abandoned you. The gods made us deluded; they must have wanted to punish you. Some gods support Troy, and they knew that you would kill many Trojans. The gods also wanted to hurt us because they knew that we could not conquer Troy without your help.

"The Fates will find their way. They bring ills and goods to mortals, and no mortal knows what the path of his life will bring. A good man may suffer many evil things. An evil man may enjoy many good things. All that we can do is, when we have evil fortune, endure the evil things, and when we have good fortune, enjoy the good things.

"We were wrong when we left you alone on the island of Lemnos. Because we were wrong, we will recompense you. Right now, we give you seven slave-women, twenty fast horses that have won prizes, and twelve tripods. These are the things that make a man wealthy. You will also always be welcome to feast in my camp with the other leading Greeks. When Troy falls, you will get additional recompense."

Agamemnon gave him the gifts, and Philoctetes said, "I am not angry at you or at any of the other Greeks. It is not good to always be angry. Often it is better to give up anger. But let us sleep now, so that we can be rested and fight fiercely tomorrow."

At dawn, the Greeks ate, fed their horses, and then prepared for war.

Philoctetes said to them, "Now let us go to war. We will tear down the walls of Troy and set fire to the city."

The Greeks put on their armor, and close together in a packed mass they went to fight the Trojans.

Chapter 10: The Death of Paris

The Trojans were outside the city, burying their dead. They saw the Greeks coming toward them, so they quickly put earth over the dead and then returned behind the walls of the city.

Polydamas, an intelligent man, said to his fellow Greeks, "Ares is raging against Troy. The war has gone on a long time, and the Greeks are fighting well. They are winning the war. I think that we should stay in our city and fight the Greeks from our walls. Eventually, they will get tired and return to their homes. Poseidon with assistance from Apollo built the walls of Troy, and the Greeks will not be able to tear down what the gods have done. We need not worry about food and drink because we have large supplies of both stored in Priam's palace. Even if large numbers of allies were to come to Troy to help us fight the Greeks, we would have enough food and drink for everybody for a long time."

Aeneas, however, replied, "Polydamas, you are wrong. You are not talking like an intelligent man. If we stay inside the city, we will be crowded and suffer much. If the Greeks have not grown tired of war and returned home in the ten years we have been fighting, they are unlikely to go home anytime soon. If we stay inside the walls of Troy, they will think that we have grown tired of war, and so the Greeks will attack even more fiercely. The stores of food and drink you mention are not as great as you suppose. If we stay shut up behind the walls of the city, we will not be able to get grain from the city of Thebe or wine from the country of Lydia. It is better for us to fight. If Zeus is opposed to us, I prefer to die quickly in battle among warriors than to die slowly of starvation among old fathers and women and young children."

The Trojans approved of the words of Aeneas. They prepared to fight outside of the city, and Zeus sent them courage. Many deaths, however, would soon occur, including the death of Paris at the hands of Philoctetes.

Eris, the goddess who values strife and discord, appeared in the battle. She wore armor that was splattered with blood, and she encouraged the warriors on both sides to fight and to die. The warriors stamped loudly on the earth as they went to war.

Aeneas killed Harpalion with a spear beneath his waist. Aeneas then killed Hyllus with a javelin to the throat. Hyllus was born on Crete, and his death pained his king, Idomeneus.

Neoptolemus killed and killed again. He killed twelve Trojans: Cebrus, Harmon, Pasitheus, Ismenus, Imbrasius, Schedius, Phleges, Mnesaeus, Ennomus, Amphinomus, Phasis, and Galenus. Galenus had brought a huge army to Troy because Priam had promised him many glorious gifts, but Galenus died before he could take those gifts home.

The Trojan Eurymenes, one of Aeneas' friends, fought fiercely. He killed many Greeks, and the Greeks retreated from him. He killed so many Greeks that he grew exhausted, and the point of his spear bent back, blunting it, and the hilt of his sword broke. Meges' spear hit him in the throat, and his blood gushed out, taking his life with it.

Two Greeks, Deilion and Amphion, started to strip Eurymenes' armor off his corpse, but Aeneas killed them. In a vineyard a man destroys wasps before they eat the fruit; Deilion and Amphion died before they had acquired the booty they desired.

Diomedes killed Menon and Amphinous, two good men.

Paris used an arrow to kill Demoleon, who had sailed to Troy under the command of Menelaus. Paris shot the arrow under Demoleon's right breast.

Teucer killed Zechis, the son of Medon. Zechis came from Phrygia, where is a cave in which the shepherd Endymion slept. Selene, the Titan Moon goddess, saw him and loved him and came down from the sky and slept with him. People today visit the cave, which is sacred to nymphs, and a stream that comes from it, and the people marvel.

The Greek Meges speared Alcaeus under the heart with his spear and sent him to the Land of the Dead. Phyllis and Margasus, the parents of Alcaeus, were never able to rejoice at their son's return home.

Little Ajax stabbed Scylaceus, one of Glaucus' friends, with a spear that reached over his shield and pierced his shoulder. The wound spurted blood over the top of his shield, but Scylaceus did not die at Troy; he was fated to die at home in Lycia after the war. He returned alone to Lycia; all the other Lycians had died in the war. Outside their city, the Lycian women asked him about their husbands and their sons, and he told them that they had all died. Angry that he alone had survived the war, they stoned him to death, and then they covered his corpse with the stones that had killed him. His tomb was near the tomb of the Lycian hero Bellerophon. After Scylaceus died, the god Apollo decreed that the mortal should be worshipped as if he were a god, and the Lycians obeyed Apollo's decree.

Philoctetes killed Deioneus and Acamas, as well as many other Trojans. He was dangerous like Ares or like a river that violently rushes downstream and floods and washes away dikes and dams. The Trojans were afraid to come close to Philoctetes, who used the weapons of Heracles.

On the belt of his quiver appeared the images of dangerous beasts: bears, jackals, leopards, wolves, boars, and lions. Blood and slaughter and battles also appeared on the war-belt.

On his quiver appeared Hermes, who was slaughtering Argus, the hundred-eyed giant. Usually, Argus' eyes took turns sleeping, but Hermes played music that put all of Argus' hundred eyes to sleep, and then Hermes killed the giant.

On his quiver also appeared Phaëthon, after he had been thrown from the chariot of the Sun-god. Phaëthon had not been able to control the immortal horses that pulled the chariot, and the Sun had come too close to the earth, burning it. Smoke came from the earth.

On his quiver also appeared Perseus, who was slaying Medusa. Anyone who looked directly at this monster would be turned to stone. Perseus cut off her head. He avoided being turned to stone by looking at her reflection in his shield, which was mirrored.

On his quiver also appeared Prometheus, who suffered terribly as an eagle ate his liver, which grew back each night so that the eagle could devour it again the following day.

The god Hephaestus had made the quiver and its belt for Heracles, who had given them to Philoctetes.

Paris shot an arrow at Philoctetes, but he narrowly missed him and instead hit Cleodorus in the shoulder. Cleodorus was retreating until he could get another shield because Polydamas had swung an ax and cut the strap of Cleodorus' shield, which had fallen to the ground. Because Cleodorus was unprotected by a shield, Paris was able to kill him.

Philoctetes said to Paris, "You should not challenge me because I will kill you. You started this war, and you have brought disaster to your city."

Philoctetes fitted an arrow to his bowstring and drew it back until his bow was almost a circle. Philoctetes' arrow grazed Paris' arm, doing little damage. Paris fitted an arrow to his bowstring, but Philoctetes was quicker and his second arrow hit Paris in his groin, forcing him to withdraw from the battle. Paris was like a dog that has been attacking a lion but is overcome with fear and runs away.

The battle continued, and warriors on both sides fell. Dying warriors fell on dead warriors.

Paris moaned because of pain as doctors attended to him, and when night approached, the two armies stopped fighting. The doctors could not stop Paris' pain, and he lay awake all night. According to a prophecy, which Paris believed, the only one who could prevent his death was his first wife, Oenone — if she were willing to help him.

Before Paris was born, his mother, Hecuba, dreamed that she would give birth to a flaming torch. Seers interpreted this to mean that her child would be the destruction of Troy, and so they advised that the child be killed. A shepherd took the infant Paris to Mount Ida, where he was supposed to lie exposed to wild animals that would kill him, but the shepherd was unwilling to leave the infant to die so he raised Paris to adulthood. When Paris was herding sheep on Mount Ida, the nymph Oenone saw him, fell in love with him, and became his first wife. She told him that she could cure any wound he suffered, no matter how serious the wound was. Later, Paris left Oenone so that he could go to Sparta and run away with Helen. Oenone mourned the end of her marriage.

Paris decided to go to Mount Ida and seek the mountain-nymphs and ask Oenone to cure his wound and save his life. The bird-signs were ominous, but Paris hoped that they were wrong.

On Mount Ida, Paris kneeled before his first wife, who was with other nymphs, and begged her to save him. The infection of his wound was spreading. Suffering pain, and growing feeble, he said to her, "My wife of long ago, do not hate me because I left you for Helen. Fate forced me to leave you. I wish that I had died in your arms before I met and slept with Helen. Have mercy on me. Use your knowledge of healing drugs to take away my pain and stop the poison of Philoctetes' arrow from killing me. You have that power, if you are willing to act. Restrain your jealousy, and heal me while there is still time. I am at your feet. The Prayers of Repentance, who sometimes seek vengeance against excessively proud people, want you to heal me. I know that I have done wrong, and I hope that you will forgive me and heal me."

Oenone was unwilling to heal him: "Why have you come to me? Why didn't you go to Helen? You abandoned me so that you could have Helen, who is rumored to be immortal, so go to her. You ignored my feelings and my mourning. You preferred Helen's bed to my bed, so go and sleep with her. You ignored my tears, and now I ignore your tears. If I could steel myself to do it, I would eat your flesh as if I were a wild animal. Where is Aphrodite? Where is Zeus, your father-in-law? Get out! You have been a disaster to Troy and the Trojans. Many gods and mortals are mourning the loss of loved ones because of you. Go to Helen and lie whimpering with pain in her bed until she cures you."

Paris was forced to leave her home. He would soon die, and Oenone would also soon die.

Paris began his journey down Mount Ida. He limped, and he suffered. Hera, who hated him, saw him and was happy. On Mount Olympus, Hera sat by four handmaidens, daughters of Selene the Moon-goddess and Helios the Sun-god. The four handmaidens manage the four seasons. Hera, an immortal goddess, knew what fate had planned after the death of Paris. Helen would marry Deiphobus, and Helenus would become angry. The Greeks would capture Helenus, still angry, who would give them information that would help Odysseus and Diomedes to enter Troy, kill Alcathous, and with Athena's consent steal the Palladium, a statue of Athena — as long as the Palladium was in Troy, the city would not fall, even if the strongest god opposed it. No mortal had created the Palladium; Zeus threw it from Mount Olympus to Troy. Hera and her four handmaidens talked about the future.

Paris did not make it to Troy and Helen; he died on Mount Ida. The nymphs who had known him when he was a young child and then an adolescent cried; they and he had been friends. Shepherds mourned with the nymphs.

A shepherd brought the news of Paris' death to Hecuba, who mourned, "You have died, my son. Except for Hector, you were my favorite of all my sons. I shall mourn you as long as I live. I am afraid that fate has more evils planned for the future. I hope that I die before I see more of my sons killed in the war, Troy conquered and burned, and my daughters and daughters-in-law and all their children made slaves and forced to serve Greek masters."

Priam, who was away, sitting and mourning by the tomb of Hector, had not yet heard of the death of his son Paris. Hector had been the best of his sons and the best Trojan warrior; he had been the main defender of Troy.

Helen loudly cried; she knew that the Trojans expected her to cry. But Helen also had private thoughts that she did not want the Trojans to know: *Paris, my husband, you have been a disaster to me. Your death is also a disaster to me. It would have been better for me if the Harpies had killed me and I had not become your wife. I am in Troy, a city where many warriors have died for me and all the citizens have suffered because of me. Now that you are gone, I have lost the husband who protected me. What will happen to me? The Trojans hate me. The Greeks hate me. If I run to the Greeks, what will they do to me? Will they rape me and then kill me? If I stay here, what will the Trojans do to me? Will the Trojan men and women kill me? Whoever kills me — Greeks or Trojans — will not give my corpse a proper burial — no earth will cover my body. I wish that I were dead; I wish that I had died before I ever came to Troy.*

Helen cried loudly. The Trojans thought that she was crying for Paris, but she was crying for herself and her sin. The Trojan women also cried loudly. People thought that the Trojan women were crying for Paris, but they were crying for husbands, sons, brothers, and fathers who had died because of Paris.

Many people cried, but most were not crying with grief at the death of Paris. Oenone alone among Paris' lovers deeply and sincerely mourned his death, but she mourned silently and did not cry. She lay in the bed that Paris and she had shared.

Oenone thought, *I fell in love with Paris, and he abandoned me for another woman. I had wanted him to stay with me until we died of old age. I wish that I had died before he abandoned me, but although he abandoned me I still love him and I want to die by his body.*

That night, while her father and the others slept, Oenone left her home and ran swiftly to the funeral-pyre of Paris. Oenone usually feared the wild animals that hunt during the night, but now she felt no fear of them. Selene, the goddess of the Moon, looked down at Oenone and knew that she was mourning the death of Paris. Selene remembered Endymion, a handsome mortal she had loved who now slept forever without aging, and she felt empathy for Oenone.

Nymphs mourned around the funeral-pyre where the corpse of Paris burned. Oenone covered her face with her clothing, and then she jumped into the fire. She willingly gave up her life.

The nymphs who had known Paris and who mourned him thought, *As an adult, Paris became foolish and wicked. He gave up a wife who loved him for a wife who has brought destruction to his family and his city and the citizens of his city.*

The bodies of Paris and Oenone burned, side by side. At Thebes, Capaneus had boasted that not even Zeus could prevent him from conquering the city. Zeus was insulted by Capaneus' impiety and killed him with a thunderbolt. As Capaneus' body was burning on a funeral-pyre, his wife, Evadne, jumped into the fire and died beside him.

After the fire had burned away the flesh of Paris and Oenone, shepherds and nymphs put out the fire with wine and gathered the bones and buried them. The shepherds and nymphs made two memorial pillars, but the pillars face away from each other, a symbol of the separation Paris and Oenone had suffered in life.

Chapter 11: Battles

The Trojan women could not go to Paris' grave to mourn his death because the gravesite lay far from the city, and the fighting continued outside the walls of Troy. The death of Paris did not end the war.

The Greeks and the Trojans fought on the plain in front of Troy. Eris, Enyo, and Ares made sure that blood spilled and warriors died — the result of spears, arrows, axes, and swords.

Neoptolemus killed Laodamas, who had been raised in Lycia by the river Xanthus, which the goddess Leto had created when, while giving birth to Apollo and Artemis, she had beat her hand on the ground, cracked it, and brought the water of the river to the surface.

Neoptolemus then killed Nirus with a spear to the jaw. The spear cut off his tongue. Nirus howled as his blood gushed out and he fell. Neoptolemus then speared and killed Evenor, Iphition, and Hippomedon. Hippomedon did not return alive to his mother, the nymph Ocyroe.

Aeneas retaliated by killing Bremon and Andromachus, who fought in chariots. Aeneas speared Bremon in the throat, and he threw a rock that hit Andromachus on his temple. Their fine horses panicked and ran over the battlefield until Aeneas' aides captured them.

Philoctetes shot an arrow that hit the back of the fleeing Peirasus' knee and lamed him. A Greek swung his sword and decapitated Peirasus. His head — its lips parted to scream — rolled far from his body.

The Trojan Polydamas speared Cleon and Eurymachus, who came to Troy with the very handsome Nireus. Cleon and Eurymachus were skilled at fishing, whether with hooks or nets or tridents.

The Greek Eurypylus killed Hellus, a Trojan ally. With his sword, Eurypylus cut off Hellus' arm, which still held a spear. The arm would have killed a Greek, but it was powerless now that it had been separated from the rest of the body.

The Greeks killed many Trojans. Odysseus killed Aenus and Polyidus. He used a spear to kill one warrior and a sword to kill the other. Sthenelus killed Abas with a javelin to the neck. Diomedes killed Laodocus, and Agamemnon killed Melius.

The Trojans killed many Greeks. Deiphobus killed Dryas and Alcimus. Agenor killed Hippasus, who grew up by the river Peneius.

The Greeks retaliated. Thoas killed Lamus and Lyncus. Meriones killed Lycon. Menelaus killed Archelochus, who used to live near a fire that never went out, around which fruit-bearing palm trees grew.

The Trojan Menoetes charged at Teucer, who shot him in the heart with an arrow. Menoetes died before Teucer's bowstring stopped vibrating.

The Greek Euryalus threw a huge stone into the ranks of the Trojans. A man can become angry at noisy cranes that threaten his crops — he uses a sling made of ox sinews to throw a stone among them, and the stone causes the cranes to become frightened and to fly away. Euryalus' throw was effective; it shattered the helmet and the head of Meles and killed him.

A strong wind can uproot trees and kill them and lay them in the dust. In the battle, warriors killed warriors and lay them in the dust.

Taking the form of the prophet Polymestor, who served him, Apollo went to Aeneas and Eurymachus and said, "Both of you are fated to live a long time, so keep fighting the Greeks."

Apollo disappeared, but Aeneas and Eurymachus recognized him and felt stronger and braver. They attacked the Greeks the way that wasps attack bees that swarm around drying grapes at harvest time. The Fates rejoiced, Ares laughed, and Enyo shrieked.

Aeneas, Eurymachus, and the other Trojans killed many Greeks. The dying Greeks were like falling grain that the reapers cut at harvest time. The battlefield was crowded with bodies and wet with blood. The Trojans were like lions attacking sheep.

The Greeks fled, and Aeneas and Eurymachus pursued and killed them. Apollo enjoyed the sight. Pigs can come into a field filled with grain because the reapers have not yet completed the harvest. Dogs chase and bite the pigs, which think no longer of food but only of escape. The pigs squeal and flee. The Greeks also fled and thought no longer of battle.

One Greek retreated no more but instead turned his horse around to fight the Trojans, but Agenor cut off the Greek's arm at the bicep with a two-edged ax. The wound spurted blood, and the Greek hung on his horse's neck and then fell to the ground. Although his arm had been severed, his hand still held on tight to the reins. The warrior was dead, but his hand and arm seemed to still want to fight.

Aeneas killed Aethalides with a spear through his back; the point of the spear came out through his navel. Aethalides fell to the ground, holding both the end of the spear and his intestines. He groaned, his teeth bit the ground, and he died.

The Greeks were like a team of oxen that have been plowing but a gadfly torments them and makes them run away, worrying the farmer who needs to get the plowing done and is also afraid that the iron plow may bounce into the air and land on the rear legs of the oxen and cut them.

Neoptolemus tried to rally the Greeks: "Be brave again. Right now you are like starlings pursued by hawks. Seek glory. Know that it is better to fight and die than to run away from a battle."

The Greeks listened to him, and he and his Myrmidons rushed upon the Trojans and killed many warriors. They pushed Aeneas and the Trojans back — a little. The goddess Enyo made the two armies equal in strength and courage and killing ability.

Neoptolemus and Aeneas fought in two different parts of the battlefield, and each killed many enemy warriors. Thetis respected Aphrodite, and she did not want her grandson to fight Aphrodite's son. The birds were eager to feast on dead warriors, but the nymphs of the Trojan rivers Simois and Xanthus mourned the deaths of Trojans.

A wind arose and blew dust into the air, reducing visibility to zero. Even so, the warriors fought and killed anyone they ran into. The dust made it impossible to tell friendly warrior from enemy warrior, and fearing to meet an enemy warrior who would immediately kill them, Trojans killed Trojans, and Greeks killed Greeks. Zeus pitied them, and he stopped the wind and the dust settled. Now, Trojans killed Greeks, and Greeks killed Trojans.

Shepherds on far-away heights watched the battle. One shepherd raised his hands and prayed to the gods that the Trojans would be victorious and drive the Greeks back to Greece, but Fate would not let this happen. Fate is powerful and can withstand even the will of Zeus. Fate determines a man's destiny, and whether his life will be good or bad. Because of Fate, the Trojans and the Greeks kept killing each other. Fate also determines a city's destiny and whether the city will rise or fall.

Athena rallied the Greeks; she was eager to see Troy fall. Aphrodite hid Aeneas with fog and took him away from the fighting. Although Aeneas was fated to survive the fall of Troy, Aphrodite was afraid that Athena might go against Fate and kill him. Earlier in the war, Athena had even fought Ares and defeated him. Ares, a god, was superior in strength to Aeneas, a mortal.

The Trojans retreated, and many warriors and horses died and many chariots were wrecked. Corpses, warriors, horses, and chariots were bloody.

A raft can be disassembled on the beach, and its logs lie on the beach and are washed by waves. Many Trojans, struck down by spears and swords, lay like logs on the battlefield and were washed by blood. They no longer thought about the agony of war.

The battle ended, and the surviving Trojans retreated behind the walls of Troy. Their wives helped take off their bloody armor and prepared hot baths for them. Doctors attended wounded warriors. The families of the wounded gathered around them and mourned, and many families mourned warriors who did not return to Troy. The Greeks also attended to their wounded.

When dawn arose, most Greeks fought again, but some Greeks stayed in the camps to guard the wounded, lest the enemy attack them.

The Trojans fought on this day from behind their walls. The Greeks Sthenelus and Diomedes fought at the Scaean Gates, which Deiphobus, Polites, and other Trojans defended with arrows and rocks. Often, flying weapons struck helmets, and the helmets protected the warriors.

Neoptolemus and his Myrmidons fought at the Idaean Gates, which Helenus, Agenor, and other Trojans courageously defended.

Odysseus and Eurypylus fought at the gates that faced the plain and ships and sea, and Aeneas opposed them.

Teucer, the Greek archer, was stationed at the gate that faced the Simois River. Trojans also defended this gate.

The warriors fighting with Odysseus arranged their shields in a pattern that Odysseus thought of. Close together, they lifted their shields and formed a roof or tortoise shell over their heads so that all the warriors were protected from arrows the way that a roof protects the inhabitants of a home from rain. The Trojans threw down weapons from their walls, and many arrows and spears stuck in the shields but the shields blunted the points of other arrows and spears and they did not stick. The weapons hitting the shields sounded like rain hitting a roof.

Under the shields, the Greeks moved to the Trojan wall, and Agamemnon and Menelaus rejoiced. The Greeks planned to reach the gates and tear them down. Their plan was good, but Aeneas seized a boulder and dropped it on the shields, which broke. The boulder crushed the warriors underneath their broken shields the way that a falling mountain crag can crush goats. Aeneas continued to drop huge rocks on the Greek warriors, and he destroyed their tortoise shell. Aeneas frightened the Greek warriors the way that mountain crags that Zeus hits with thunderbolts and sends crashing down the mountain frighten shepherds and sheep.

Aeneas' armor gleamed so brightly that no one could look at him, and he had the strength of a god. Ares stood beside him and guided the rocks that Aeneas dropped to ensure that they caused maximum loss of life. Aeneas was fighting the way that Zeus fought when he destroyed the rebelling Titans. The Trojans had carried many rocks to the top of their walls, and Aeneas used these to destroy the Greeks and protect his city.

The Trojans fought courageously beside Aeneas. He rallied the Trojans, ordering them to fight for their city, their children, their wives, their parents, and themselves. Neoptolemus ordered the Myrmidons to fight to conquer Troy and burn it.

Little Ajax, fighting away from the section of wall that Aeneas defended, killed many Trojans with his arrows and javelins. He killed so many Trojans that they abandoned the wall. Alcimedon, a Locrian warrior under Little Ajax' command, climbed a scaling ladder while holding his shield over his head. He climbed to the top of the wall and looked down on the city, but Aeneas saw him and brought a rock down on him. The rock hit Alcimedon and also broke the ladder he was climbing. Alcimedon's helmet fell from his head, and he dropped his shield and spear as he fell to his doom. Alcimedon's brain splattered when he hit the ground, and his bones broke through his skin.

Philoctetes aimed an arrow at Aeneas, but his shield protected him with the aid of Aeneas' mother, Aphrodite. The arrow barely grazed the shield and then hit Mimas, who fell from the Trojan wall just like a goat falls from a mountain crag after an archer hits it with an arrow.

Angry at the death of Mimas, Aeneas threw a rock that shattered the skull of Toxaichmes, who was one of Philoctetes' friends.

Philoctetes shouted at Aeneas, "You think that you are a brave warrior, but you are fighting from a wall like a woman would fight. If you are brave, come out onto the battlefield and fight me."

Aeneas did not reply, although he wanted to. He was too busy fighting to defend his city. He and the Trojans had been fighting for ten years, and they were still fighting.

Chapter 12: The Trojan Horse

When the battle ended, Troy had still not fallen, and the prophet Calchas called the Greek leaders to a meeting so that he could tell them what he had learned from Apollo. Calchas had the ability to clearly remember the past, clearly see the present, and partially predict the future.

Calchas told the Greek leaders, "Let us not fight the Trojans directly, but instead conceive of a trick to fool the Trojans and so at last conquer Troy. Yesterday, I watched a hawk hunt a dove. The dove, frightened, went into a hole in a rock. The hawk waited outside the hole for a long time, but the dove saw it and stayed in the hole. Then the hawk hid itself in a bush near the hole. The dove waited a while, and then came out of the hole, thinking that the hawk had flown away. The hawk then caught and killed the dove. Let us think up a trick that will result in the fall of Troy."

The Greek leaders thought for a long time, and then clever Odysseus said, "Here is a way that we can conquer the city through trickery. We can build a giant wooden horse; it will be hollow so that warriors can hide inside it. Our fleet will sail away and hide behind the nearby island of Tenedos so the Trojans cannot see our ships. When the ships sail away, we Greeks will burn our camps so that the Trojans think that we are really gone. One brave Greek must stay and allow the Trojans to capture him. He must tell the Trojans that he escaped from the Greeks because they wanted to kill him as a human sacrifice so that they would have safe returns to their homes. He must convince the Trojans to pull the horse inside their city by telling them that according to a prophecy as long as the horse is inside the city, Troy will not fall. The brave Greek must tell the Trojans that the Greeks made the horse for the goddess Athena, who is angry at the Greeks. The brave Greek must stand up to the Trojans' questioning, which will be harsh, until they believe his story and take him and the horse inside Troy. At night, when it is safe and the Trojans are sleeping, the brave Greek will tell the warriors to come out of the horse and make their way to the Trojan gates and open them. The brave Greek can use a burning torch to signal the warriors on the ships, which will have returned to the Trojan shore, to come to the gates. The Greek warriors inside Troy will open the gates and let in our army so that we can finally conquer Troy."

The Greeks, and especially Calchas, approved of Odysseus' plan. Calchas marveled at Odysseus' cleverness.

Calchas advised the Greek leaders, "Let us follow Odysseus' plan, which omens show will be successful. We can hear the thunder and see the lightning of Zeus, and birds have been shrieking to the right of our troops — the lucky side. This trick is exactly what we need, as the Trojans are desperate and so are fighting better than ever. Even a coward can fight fiercely when it is necessary to save his life. Fighting even fiercer than that is a man who is desperate to save his parents, wife, children, and city — such a man is willing to die if necessary to save his loved ones. A desperate enemy is a dangerous enemy."

Two men, Neoptolemus and Philoctetes, opposed the plan. They had recently come to Troy and were not yet exhausted from the fighting. They were eager to gain glory in war.

Neoptolemus said, "Brave men fight their enemy face to face. Cowardly men fight from the walls of their city. We are braver than the Trojans, and we ought to seek glory on the battlefield. Let us conquer Troy through battle and not through trickery."

Odysseus replied, "Neoptolemus, I respect you and I respected your father. You are and he was a brave and noble man. Achilles, however, despite all his strength and courage and fighting ability, was unable to conquer Troy. And all of the many experienced warriors here have been unable to conquer Troy, although we have been fighting with all our strength for ten years. So let us follow the advice of Calchas. We can have Epeus, our best carpenter, design and build the horse. Athena taught him what he knows."

The Greeks, except for Neoptolemus and Philoctetes, approved the plan. Neoptolemus and Philoctetes planned to continue to fight on the battlefield, but the actions of Zeus convinced them not to fight. Zeus caused an earthquake and threw a thunderbolt that landed in front of Neoptolemus and Philoctetes. They knew that they had offended Zeus, and so they agreed to Odysseus' plan. They realized that Calchas knew the will of Zeus.

That night, Athena appeared in the guise of a young girl to Epeus in a dream. Athena told him how to design and make the horse. She also told him that she would be near him as he made the horse and that she would help him. Epeus woke up, and he knew that he would follow the goddess' directions. He could think of nothing other than the horse.

At dawn, Epeus gave the Greek leaders pleasure when he told them about his dream and about Athena's directions for designing and making the horse.

Agamemnon and Menelaus ordered the Greeks to go to Mount Ida and fell trees for lumber to build the horse. They clear-cut a wide area that had housed many wild animals; the animals did not like the area after it was clear-cut.

The Greeks cut up the trees into long sections, and men and mules carried them to Epeus. They cut the timber into planks, and Epeus supervised them in how to build the horse. Each Greek who was not standing guard found something to do to help build the horse. They built the feet and legs and then the belly of the horse. Then they built the flanks and back and throat and head. Epeus added a mane and a tail and ears and eyes. In three days, the horse was finished.

Epeus prayed, "Athena, here is your horse, made according to your directions. May you keep it and me, who will be inside it, safe."

Athena listened to his prayer. He had created a work of art as well as a weapon of destruction, and she knew that she would answer his prayer.

While the Greeks admired the horse and the Trojans stayed behind the walls of their city, Zeus left Mount Olympus and visited lands far away. Without Zeus present to maintain peace, the other gods split into two factions: those who supported the Greeks and those who supported the Trojans. The gods came down from Mount Olympus to the river Xanthus and took up opposing positions on each side of the river. Many minor sea-gods took up positions alongside the Olympian gods. Some gods wanted to destroy the horse and the ships, and other gods wanted to destroy Troy, but Fate made them turn their hatred against each other. Ares attacked Athena, and all the other gods began to fight. The sounds of the gods' battle reached the Land of the Dead and terrified the Titans, but the living mortals were unaware that the gods were fighting.

In their battle, the gods broke off mountain crags and threw them at each other, but the crags broke against the gods' immortal bodies. Zeus became aware of the gods' battle. Iris yoked the four winds to Zeus' chariot, and Zeus drove it to Mount Olympus and then threw thunderbolts at the site of the gods' battle. The gods were terrified.

The goddess of justice, Themis, who alone of the gods had refrained from fighting, went down to the gods and said, "Stop fighting. Zeus does not want you to fight. It is hardly right for immortals, who live forever, to fight over mortals, who live only a short time. Being immortal, you are vulnerable to eternal punishment. If Zeus wishes, he can cover you with a mountain. For the rest of your lives, which last forever, you will see only darkness."

The gods listened to Themis and stopped fighting. Some gods stayed on the land, and the others returned to the sky or the sea.

After the horse had been completed, Odysseus said to the Greeks, "We have some decisions to make. Who will be the warriors who will go inside the horse? Who will be the warriors who will sail behind the island of Tenedos and hide their presence from the Trojans? Most importantly, who will be the brave Greek who will stay behind and allow the Trojans to capture him so that he can convince the Trojans to pull the horse inside the city as a gift to Athena? That Greek should not be well known to the Trojans. All of the Greeks whom the Trojans know well will be great warriors who have killed many men, and if the Trojans capture one of these Greeks, the Trojans will immediately kill him."

Sinon spoke up: "Odysseus, I am willing to be the man whom the Trojans capture. I realize that they may torture me and may kill me. They may even throw me — while I am still alive — into a fire, but I am willing to suffer all this. I want to bring us glory, and I want us to conquer Troy."

The Greeks were impressed by his bravery. One Greek said, "Sinon has not been this courageous before, but he is definitely very courageous now. Troy is doomed."

Nestor said, "I wish that I could be the first warrior to go inside the horse. When I was young and Jason summoned the Argonauts, I wanted to be the first warrior to go inside the *Argo*, but Pelias, my uncle, stopped me from enjoying that honor. Now, although I am old, I will gladly go inside the horse."

Neoptolemus said, "Nestor, you are the wisest of all of the Greeks, but you are old now and you have lost much of your strength. You must be one of those who sail behind the island of Tenedos. Younger men, including myself, will go inside the horse and do the deeds that you would like to do."

Nestor kissed Neoptolemus' hands and head. He was pleased with what Neoptolemus had said. Neoptolemus was eager to win glory, and he had shown concern and respect for Nestor, an old man.

Nestor said to Neoptolemus, "You are truly the son of Achilles, both in strength and in intelligence. Now that you are fighting for us, we will conquer

Troy. It will have taken ten years, but the gods force us to work hard before we gain good things."

Neoptolemus replied, "I also hope that we conquer Troy, but if the gods will not allow that to happen, I prefer to die here rather than to return home in disgrace."

Neoptolemus put on his armor. So did the other Greek warriors who would go inside the horse.

Muses, tell me the names of the brave Greeks who entered the horse. The first to enter the horse was Neoptolemus, and he was followed by Menelaus, Odysseus, Sthenelus, Diomedes, Philoctetes, Anticlus, Menestheus, Thoas, Polypoetes, Little Ajax, Eurypylus, Thrasymedes, Meriones, Idomeneus, Podalirius, Eurymachus, Teucer, Ialmenus, Thalpius, Antimachus, Leonteus, Eumelus, Euryalus, Demophoon, Amphimachus, Agapenor, Acamas, and Meges. Other outstanding warriors also went inside the horse. The last to go inside the horse was Epeus, who had designed it with the help of Athena. Epeus entered last because he would open one of the two doors at the right time. Odysseus would open the other door. They drew inside the horse the ladders they had used, and they closed the doors. Soon, the Greeks inside the horse would either die or they would conquer Troy.

The other Greeks burned their camps, and then they sailed away to Tenedos. Nestor and Agamemnon commanded these Greeks. Both Nestor and Agamemnon had wanted to go inside the horse, but the other Greeks vetoed that idea. Commanders were needed for the Greek fleet. Behind Tenedos, the Greeks cast their anchors and waited on shore. The next night, Sinon would burn a torch on the wall of Troy, and the Greeks would know that they should go to the gates of Troy.

Inside the horse, the Greeks sometimes thought of dying and they sometimes thought of burning the city.

At dawn, the Trojans saw smoke still rising from the Greek camps. They did not see the Greeks' ships. Despite their joy, they put on their armor before going to the Greek camps. They also saw the horse and admired it.

The Trojans captured Sinon. They surrounded him, and they asked him questions. At first, they were gentle, and then they were not gentle. They wanted to make sure that he told them the truth. They cut off his nose and his ears, and they tortured him with fire, but Sinon was brave and he continued to lie. They asked him where were the Greeks and if anything was inside the horse. Because he was brave and lied, the Trojans did not find out about the Greeks inside the horse — if Sinon had told the truth, those Greeks would have died.

Sinon told the Trojans, "The Greeks have given up. They have sailed away to their homes. Calchas told the Greeks that Athena is angry at them because Odysseus and Diomedes stole from Troy the statue of Athena that is known as the Palladium; the Greeks built the horse as an offering to Athena so that she will stop being angry at them. The Greeks also wanted to kill me. Odysseus told the Greeks that to ensure their safe passage home they needed to make me a human sacrifice to the gods of the sea. I learned of this plot, and I took sanctuary at the feet of the horse. I was under the protection of Athena, and so the Greeks could not kill me. If they had killed me, they would have further enraged Athena."

So Sinon spoke, and he spoke persuasively. Some Trojans believed him; however, other Trojans did not believe him.

Laocoon was one of the Trojans who did not believe him. He told the Trojans that the horse was a trick of the Greeks, and he advised the Trojans to burn the horse and see if anything were hidden inside it.

Athena came to the aid of the Greeks. She caused an earthquake under the feet of Laocoon, and she caused pain in his eyes. His eyes rolled, and ooze and blood flowed from them. While he could still see, he saw double, and then Athena entirely took away his sight. Despite being now completely blind, he was concerned for his city and continued to urge the Trojans to burn the horse.

The Trojans pitied Laocoon, and they feared Athena, whom they believed that Laocoon had offended. They also worried that they had offended Athena by torturing Sinon, so they welcomed him.

Sinon told them that according to a prophecy if the Trojans took the horse inside the city, it would never fall. By taking the horse inside Troy, they could make it their own offering to Athena. The Trojans believed him, and they put a rope around the horse and pulled it to the city. Epeus had put wheels under the horse to make it easier to pull.

As the Trojans pulled the horse into the city as if they were pulling a ship into water, they celebrated what they believed to be their victory in the war. They put garlands on the horse, and they wore garlands on their heads. They played flutes. The goddesses Enyo, Hera, and Athena laughed because they knew that the war was coming to an end with the Greeks victorious.

Epeus had made the horse huge. It would not fit through the gates, but the Trojans tore down some of their own battlements so that they could bring the horse inside Troy. The Trojan women stared at the horse; they did not know that soon many of them would die and others would become slaves.

Laocoon continued to try to convince the Trojans to burn the horse, but the Trojans were convinced that doing that would anger the gods. They became even more convinced of that when Athena sent two sea-snakes to kill the two sons of Laocoon. The sea-snakes swam to Troy from the island of Calydna. Aphrodite and the nymphs of the rivers Xanthus and Simois, all of whom supported the Trojans during the war, mourned.

The Trojans — men and women — fled when the sea-snakes clambered on shore. Some women were so frightened that when they fled they left their children behind. The Trojans also left behind blind Laocoon. The two boys stretched out their hands to their father as the sea-snakes seized them in their jaws, but he could not help them. After devouring the two boys, the sea-snakes vanished underground. The Trojans built a cenotaph — an empty tomb — for the two boys, and Laocoon wept. The boys' mother also wept, like a mother nightingale mourning when a snake devours her young. The boys' mother also wept for her blinded husband.

The Trojans attempted to sacrifice to the gods, but their fires went out as if rain were falling on them. The libations of wine the Trojans poured to the gods turned to blood. The floors of temples in Troy became slick from blood, and tears flowed from statues. Happy with their supposed victory, the Trojans ignored the bad omens.

One Trojan clearly saw the future: Cassandra. She had promised to sleep with Apollo if he would give her the gift of prophecy. Apollo kept his promise, but she did not keep her promise. Therefore, to punish her, Apollo gave her an additional "gift": Although Cassandra would have the gift of prophecy, no one would believe her prophecies until they had come true.

Cassandra saw the omens, and she knew what they meant. With her hair falling on her shoulders and her eyes glaring and her head turning from side to side, she said to the Trojans, "I see destruction, fire, blood, and death. I see bad omens, and yet you are celebrating. I see that your doom is hidden from you

— you cannot see it. The destruction that Helen has been bringing to Troy will finally be fulfilled. You are eating a feast, and it will be your last one. Soon, you will complete your journey to the Land of the Dead."

One of the Trojans, who like all the Trojans did not believe her prophecies, said to her, "Cassandra, stop talking nonsense. The gods have finally shown favor to us, and it would be wrong for us to reject their gifts. If you want to make dire prophecies, make them silently, to yourself. Otherwise, you may suffer a fate worse than that of Laocoon."

Cassandra wanted to destroy the horse with an ax or with fire. She picked up a burning brand from the fire and ran to the horse with a double ax in her other hand, but the Trojans stopped her and warned her to stay away from the horse and not to cause any more trouble. The Trojans then returned to their feasting.

Inside the horse, the Greeks listened to the sounds of celebrating and of drinking. They had heard the prophecy of Cassandra, and they had heard the Trojans stop her from destroying the horse. The Greeks marveled at her intelligence.

Cassandra stayed away from the horse like a lioness that has been driven away by armed shepherds and their dogs, and she mourned.

Chapter 13: The Fall of Troy

That night, the Trojans celebrated. They played music, danced, feasted, and drank wine. They became drunk, and they could not see well — everything seemed to be in motion. Drunken men cannot fight well.

The celebrating Trojans said, "The Greeks brought many warriors here, but they did not win the war. They left as if they were children or women, not warriors."

Very late that night, the Trojans slept, and Sinon displayed a blazing torch on the high walls of Troy, alerting Agamemnon and the other Greeks to return to the city. Sinon worried that the Trojans might see him, but they were all asleep. He also went to the horse and called softly to the warriors inside that it was safe to come out. The Greek warriors inside the horse had stayed awake all night. Odysseus, who warned the Greeks to be quiet, and Epeus opened the two doors of the horse and looked to see if any Trojans were awake. Some Greeks were tempted to jump out of the horse, but Odysseus restrained them with words. Alert for enemies, Odysseus was the first Greek to exit the horse. The other Greek warriors followed him. They were like wasps exiting their nest to attack a woodcutter. They made their way to the gates, killing Trojans as they went.

Meanwhile, the Greek ships had sailed back to Troy with the help of a wind sent by Thetis and had marched silently to the gates, which Sinon, Odysseus, and the others opened. They entered Troy the way that wolves enter a sheepfold, and they began to kill and kill again. They also set many buildings on fire.

Many Trojans were killed before they could put on armor and get weapons. They lay in their own blood, and dying Trojans fell on top of them. Some Trojans were grievously wounded but not dead — they fled, holding their intestines in their hands. The Greeks hacked off the feet and hands and heads of other Trojans. Many Trojans were speared in the back as they fled. In the city, dogs howled and wounded Trojans screamed.

The women also wailed. An eagle can fly among cranes and frighten them. The cranes have no courage to fight the eagle; they merely make cries of distress. So did many Trojan women. In their distress, and with many of their homes on fire, the Trojan women were not fully dressed. Many wore only a single garment, and many were naked, concealing their nakedness with only their hands. The women tore their hair and beat their breasts and cried. Some women grabbed weapons and fought the Greeks; they wanted to help their husbands and save their children.

Children woke up. Some had had nightmares in which they had died; those nightmares came true for many children. The children were like pigs being slaughtered for a feast that a rich man is holding.

Blood sprayed into the air and fell into the wine still left in mixing bowls. Trojan men, women, and children died. The swords of all the Greeks — even the worst fighters — were red with Trojan blood.

Some unarmed Trojans threw up their hands in an attempt to stop Greek swords; the swords cut off their fingers. Other unarmed Trojans reached for swords they could use to defend themselves; the Greeks used their own swords to cut off the fingers of the Trojans.

Greeks also suffered wounds, and some died. The Trojans fought back with whatever weapons they could find. They threw goblets and burning pieces of wood from the fire. The Trojans stabbed some Greeks with the spits that the Trojans had used to cook food. Some Trojans had gotten real weapons such as hatchets and battleaxes and swords and spears; they used them to kill Greeks. Many Greeks died.

In the confused fighting, sometimes a man threw a rock and killed a friend, although many Greeks carried burning torches so they could tell friend from foe.

The Trojan Coroebus attacked Diomedes, who speared him in the throat. The previous day, Coroebus had arrived at Troy. He had promised Priam to fight and to defeat the Greeks in return for a marriage to Cassandra. Diomedes then killed Eurydamas, the next Trojan to attack him.

Aged Trojans wandered or hid in the confusion. Diomedes met the aged Ilioneus, who fell to his knees and grabbed Diomedes' sword and knees. Afraid to die, Ilioneus said to him, "Have mercy on me, whoever you are. If you kill a young man in battle, you win glory, but if you kill an old man, you do not win glory. Therefore, let me live. Hope that you will also reach an advanced old age."

Diomedes replied, "I hope to live long enough to grow old, but on this day I will spare no Trojan. The Trojans are my enemies, and I will send as many of them as I can to the Land of the Dead."

Diomedes thrust his sword into Ilioneus' throat, and then he continued to kill as many Trojans as he could, including Abas and Eurycoon.

The other Greeks also killed Trojans. Little Ajax killed Amphimedon. Agamemnon killed the son of Damastor. Idomeneus killed Mimas. Meges killed Deiopites.

Neoptolemus killed Pammon, Polites, and Antiphonus — all three were sons of Priam. Then Neoptolemus killed Agenor. Neoptolemus killed many other Trojan heroes.

Neoptolemus saw Priam by the altar of Zeus in the courtyard of the palace. Priam was unafraid; he wanted to join his sons in death. Priam said to Neoptolemus, "Son of Achilles, kill me. Do not pity me because after all that my city and I have suffered and suffer, this is a good time to die. I only wish that Achilles had killed me before I ever saw my city conquered. Please kill me now so that I may no longer suffer."

Neoptolemus replied, "Yes, I will kill you because you are my enemy and life is the most valuable thing that a man can possess."

Neoptolemus swung his sword and cut off Priam's head, which rolled on the ground far from his body. Priam no longer grieved.

The innocent suffer in war. Hector had killed many Greeks, and in revenge the Greeks forcibly took Hector's toddler son, Astyanax, away from Hector's screaming wife, Andromache, and killed him by throwing him from the high walls of Troy. Astyanax had hurt no one and knew nothing of war.

The Greeks then forced Andromache to go with the other captive Trojan women. Andromache's father, husband, and son had died because of war, and now she knew that she would be a sex-slave to a Greek master — she did not yet know which one.

Andromache said to the Greeks, "Kill me now. Throw me from the high walls of Troy the way you did my toddler son. Or throw me off a cliff or into fire. Achilles killed my father in Thebe, and he killed my husband at Troy. I still had my son, but now he is dead, too. Please don't make me a sex-slave. Kill me and end my life and my misery."

The Greeks ignored her wish; she was more valuable to them alive. They dragged her away with the other Trojan women to make them slaves.

The Greeks did not burn the home of Antenor, and they did not kill him. Antenor, an advocate of peace and the husband of the priestess Theano, had wanted the Trojans to return Helen to the Greeks. When Menelaus and Odysseus had come as emissaries to the Trojans, Antenor had given them hospitality and made sure that they were safe. In return, the Greeks spared him and his house as they conquered the city. In this instance, the Greeks did what Themis, goddess of justice, wanted them to do, although they committed atrocities in other parts of Troy.

Aeneas had been fighting bravely and had killed many Greeks as he defended the doomed city, but now he realized that the city had fallen and no one could change its fate. When a large ship sinks, a sailor can take refuge in a small boat. Aeneas gave up trying to save his city and instead concentrated on saving his family.

Aeneas carried his aged father on his shoulders and he led his young son by the hand as he took them out of Troy. His son was frightened and cried as he ran beside his father. As they fled the city, Aeneas stepped over many dead bodies, and he stepped on many dead bodies.

The Greeks saw Aeneas and shot arrows and threw spears at him, but Calchas, the prophet, told them, "Stop! Aeneas is destined to survive the fall of Troy and to go to the river Tiber in Italy, where he shall become the ancestor of a mighty people who will rule the world from the east to the west. His mother is Aphrodite, and he will become a god. He deserves this destiny. In fleeing from Troy, he chose not to take gold but instead to take his aged father and his young son."

The Greeks stopped trying to kill Aeneas. His mother, Aphrodite, led him, his father, and his son safely out of the burning city.

After the death of Paris, Deiphobus had married Helen. During the fall of Troy, she hid, and Menelaus found Deiphobus drunk and still asleep in the bed he shared with Helen. Menelaus stabbed Deiphobus with a sword, and as the blood gushed out of the wound, Menelaus said, "I have killed you, and I wish that I had killed Paris, too. But both of you are dead, and you have paid your debt to Themis, goddess of justice."

Menelaus continued to kill Trojans. He wanted justice because the Trojans had done evil actions: Paris had stolen his host's wife and had stolen much of his host's treasure, the Trojans had broken oaths they had sworn to the gods, and they had killed many Greeks. Themis would not allow their city to remain unconquered.

Menelaus searched the palace and finally found Helen. He wanted to kill her, but Aphrodite filled his heart with passion, not anger. Aphrodite did not want Helen to die. Menelaus thought of marriage, not of murder. But he rushed at Helen with a sword because he wanted to show the Greeks that he knew that Helen had been the cause of so many Greek deaths. As Menelaus knew would happen, Agamemnon restrained him and did not allow him to kill Helen. The Greeks had fought a war to regain Helen, not to kill her.

Agamemnon said to Menelaus, "It is not right to kill your wife. Blame Paris, not Helen. Paris is the one who violated the rules of hospitality and treated you, his host, so badly. It is because of Paris that the gods have caused Troy to fall."

As Agamemnon had requested, Menelaus spared the life of Helen.

Many gods mourned the fall of Troy, but Athena and Hera rejoiced in its fall. But even Athena ended up feeling pain during the city's fall. Cassandra had taken refuge in the temple of Athena. The Greeks could and should have respected Athena by respecting all who took refuge in her temple — they should not kill or harm them because those inside Athena's temple were under the protection of Athena. But blinded by lust, Little Ajax committed an atrocity: He desecrated Athena's temple by going inside it and raping Cassandra. Athena averted her eyes from the rape, and she planned death for Little Ajax — he would never return home.

The city was burning, and tall buildings were falling. The houses of Aeneas and of Antimachus were burning. Temples and altars burned. Troy's destruction was assured.

The Greeks killed many Trojans, but others died in the fires. Burning buildings fell and became tombs. Some Trojans committed suicide with their own swords. Some killed their wives and children to prevent them from becoming slaves, and then they took their own lives and fell on the corpses of the family members they had killed.

One Trojan thought that the fighting was still far from his home. He took a jar to get water, hoping to be able to drink his fill before fleeing, but a Greek saw him and speared him and killed him. The still-empty jar fell and broke. Many Trojans died in their own halls when burning beams fell on them. Some women had run out of their homes when they heard the tumult of fighting and of fires; they ran back inside to get their children, and the women and children died when the burning roofs collapsed on them.

Dogs and horses ran in terror throughout the city. The horses trampled many people and killed them.

The fires that were destroying Troy could be seen from far away. From a distance, people saw the fires and knew that Troy had fallen. A sailor at sea said, "The Greeks have done a notable deed. The Trojans have paid the price for taking Helen."

A forest fire panics or kills all the wild animals living in it. All of the citizens of Troy were panicked or killed. The gods looked upon the destruction.

Theseus had once abducted the very young Helen and taken her to his home in Aphidnae, and he left her there when he visited the Land of the Dead. Helen's brothers, Castor and Polydeuces, rescued her and captured Theseus' mother, Aethra, and made her a slave. When Paris and Helen sailed to Troy, they took Aethra with them.

Aethra now was looking for Greeks. Two Greeks, Demophoon and Acamas, now saw her, and they thought that she was Hecuba, the wife of Priam. They seized her and were going to take her to the Trojan women who had been captured, but she said to them, "I am Aethra, and I am not Trojan, but Greek. I am the mother of the famous Greek hero Theseus. If you can, take me to his two sons who are at Troy. They are the same age as you, and they will be happy to see me."

Demophoon and Acamas were the two sons of Theseus at Troy, and they were happy to see her. They remembered the stories about how Castor and Polydeuces had conquered Aphidnae so they could rescue Helen. At the time, Demophoon and Acamas had been infants, and they had been safely and secretly taken away from the city. They also remembered that Aethra, their grandmother, had been made a slave and had been taken to Troy.

Demophoon said to Aethra, "Your request is granted — and quickly. We are your grandsons, and we will take care of you. We will take you to our ship, and we will take you back to Greece and freedom and family."

Aethra kissed the shoulders, head, chest, and bearded cheeks of Demophoon, and then she did the same to Acamas. A man may erroneously be reported to have died in a foreign land. He returns home, and his sons cry with pleasure at seeing him again, and the man cries, too. Such crying is pleasant. Aethra, Demophoon, and Acamas cried with pleasure.

Other kinds of crying took place in Troy. Laodice, one of the daughters of Priam, cried and lifted her arms as she prayed to the gods to let the earth open and swallow her so that she would cease living and not become a sex-slave. One of the gods answered her prayer.

The constellation named the Pleiades has seven stars, one of which is very faint. The Pleiades used to be nymphs, but Zeus made them stars and put them in the night sky. All seven stars used to be bright, but one of the stars, Electra, was the mother of Dardanus, an ancestor of the Trojans. When Troy fell, Electra dimmed herself because of her grief.

That night, the Greeks continued causing death and destruction in Troy. Eris, goddess of strife, enjoyed the deaths and the destruction.

Chapter 14: The Departure for Greece

Dawn arrived, and the Greeks looted the destroyed city, finding and taking much treasure. Along with the material treasure, they took the women of Troy. Some were virgins, others were newlyweds, others were aged and with grey hair, and others were mothers whose children had suckled their breasts for the last time. Many children had died, and many still-living children were separated from their mothers.

Menelaus took Helen, over whom the war had been fought. Agamemnon took Cassandra, and Neoptolemus took Andromache. Odysseus dragged away Hecuba, who was crying and trembling. She had torn her hair and had poured ashes on her head. Each Greek hero had a Trojan woman to take to his ships.

The Trojan women were now slaves, and they cried as their new masters led them to the ships. With the arrival of winter, men separate piglets from their mothers and drive the piglets from the old pigsty to a new pigsty. The piglets squeal as they are herded from one place to a new place. The Trojan women wailed as they were herded to the ships.

Helen did not cry, but she was afraid that the Greeks would hurt her. She covered her face with the veil of a married woman and followed her husband, Menelaus. Hephaestus had once found his wife, Aphrodite, having an affair with Ares. He cast a net over them while they were having sex, and then he invited the gods and goddesses to look at them. The goddesses were embarrassed and stayed away, but the gods came to look and laugh while Aphrodite blushed with shame. Helen blushed. The Greeks marveled at Helen's beauty, and no one insulted or physically mistreated her.

The Greeks were happy to see Helen; they had fought a war for ten years to recover her. They were like sailors who have been at sea for a long time and finally see land.

But the river-gods around Troy and their daughters the nymphs mourned, as did the god of Mount Ida, as the city was abandoned. Its buildings had been burnt, its warriors had been killed, and its surviving women and children were being taken away to be slaves in Greece. The river-gods and nymphs and mountain-god felt as a farmer does whose ripe grain field is destroyed by a hailstorm. Food that could have nourished and kept alive many people is destroyed, and the center of civilization that was Troy had been destroyed.

The Greeks sang epic songs as they went about their work of putting their booty in their ships. The songs were about the gods, the war, the wooden horse, and the Greeks' decisive victory after ten years of inconclusive warfare. The songs were joyful, like those of jackdaws following a storm when the Sun comes out. The songs reached Mount Olympus, and they made the gods who had supported the Greeks happy, but the gods who had supported the Trojans were unhappy at the working of Fate, which even they could not alter. Even Zeus, the most powerful of all beings, cannot alter Fate.

The Greeks made many sacrifices to the gods, and they praised all who had entered the wooden horse. They also especially gave gifts to and praised Sinon, who had told the lies that conquered Troy although the Trojans had tortured him in an attempt to make him tell the truth. Although the Trojans had cut off his nose and his ears, Sinon was happy with the glory that he had won.

The Greeks said among themselves, "We have won the war after ten years of struggle. We have won glory. Now we pray to Zeus to allow us a safe homecoming."

To some Greeks Zeus gave a safe homecoming, but not to all.

During the evening, poets continued to sing the history of the Trojan War: the Greek ships had gathered at Aulis, the port from which they had sailed to Troy; Achilles had sacked twenty-three cities, twelve by sea and eleven by land; Achilles had wounded Telephus, and he had killed Eetion and Cycnus; Achilles had grown angry at Agamemnon and stopped fighting for the Greeks, and the Trojans had won major battles; Achilles had killed Hector, and then he had dragged the corpse around Troy; Achilles had killed Penthesilea and Memnon, Great Ajax had killed Glaucus, and Neoptolemus had killed Eurypylus; Philoctetes had returned to fight for the Greeks and had killed Paris; Odysseus had come up with the idea of the Trojan Horse, Epeus had built it, and many Greek warriors had gone inside the horse; the Greeks had conquered Troy, and now they were celebrating.

At midnight, exhausted from the work of war and after many hours without sleep, most of the Greeks slept.

Menelaus and Helen, however, talked. Helen said, "Menelaus, do not be angry at me. Paris kidnapped me while you were away from our home; I did not go with him voluntarily. I suffered, and I wanted to commit suicide either with a noose or with a sword. The Trojans stopped me and tried with words to make me forget my sorrow at being separated from my family. I wanted to return to you and our daughter. Please believe me."

Menelaus replied, "Let us talk of this no longer. Let us forget the evil past."

Helen was relieved; her husband did not sound angry at her. She embraced him, and they lay down together, and they had sex. They were like ivy and a vine that grow together and intertwine. The wind cannot separate the ivy and the vine, and Menelaus and Helen were one.

That night, Achilles appeared in a dream to his son, Neoptolemus. Achilles kissed his son's neck and eyes, and then he said, "Do not mourn me — my spirit lives now among the gods. Let me give you some advice. During war, fight in the front lines. During councils, listen to the older men. Find men with good and noble minds, and make them your friends. Be friends with good men, and reject bad men. Make your mind good, and your deeds will be good. Pursue excellence and its rewards, and do not over-react to bad fortune or to good fortune. Be good to your friends, your future sons, and your future wife, and realize that not long from now you will be dead. Be kind.

"And do what I tell you to do now. I want you to go to Agamemnon and the other Greeks and tell them that I — who did so many notable deeds in the war — am angry at them. I am even angrier at them than I was when Agamemnon took Briseis away from me. I am so angry that I will send storms to the sea so that the Greeks will have to stay at Troy for a long time. The only way they can appease my anger is to sacrifice Polyxena, a young daughter of Priam, at my tomb. After she is dead, you may bury her at a distance from my tomb."

Achilles' spirit departed and went to the Elysian Fields, where the gods use a path that travels to and from heaven.

Neoptolemus woke up and wondered, *Some of what my father said seems contradictory. Have I heard both true things and false things? Is Achilles trying to be a good person but letting his anger conquer him? Should a good son obey his father no matter what?*

At dawn, Neoptolemus remembered the dream of his father and felt glad. The Greeks wanted to pull their ships into the sea and set sail, but Neoptolemus told the Greek leaders, "My father, Achilles, whose spirit now resides with the gods, came to me in a dream last night. He demands his share of the spoils of Troy. He orders us to sacrifice Polyxena at his tomb and then bury her at a distance from his tomb. If we don't do that, he threatens to send storms to the sea and force us to stay at Troy for a long time."

The Greeks looked out at the sea; a storm was rising and making the waves dangerous. Poseidon, who respected Achilles, had created the storm. The Greeks prayed to Achilles, and they said, "Achilles, who was descended from Zeus, is now an immortal god."

The Greeks forcibly tore Polyxena away from her mother, Hecuba, and led her to Achilles' tomb the way they would take a frightened calf from its grieving mother and lead it to an altar. Polyxena and Hecuba both knew that the Greeks were going to cut Polyxena's throat with a sword. Polyxena cried the way a mother cries when her young daughter is being taken away to be a human sacrifice. Polyxena's tears soaked her dress.

The previous night, Hecuba had had a dream: She was standing at the tomb of Achilles, crying, and from the breasts that had fed her children came not white milk but red blood that dripped onto the tomb of Achilles. She mourned the way a mother dog mourns when its masters have taken its puppies, whose eyes are still closed, and thrown them into a field for birds to kill and eat. The dog howls, and Hecuba sobbed loudly with grief.

Hecuba said, "What should I mourn first, and what should I mourn last? My sons have died. My husband has died. My city has fallen. My daughters are or will be dead, or they will be sex-slaves. You, Polyxena, will soon be dead. You are at the age where you should be looking forward to your marriage, but fate has brought you death. Achilles is dead, but that has not stopped him from bringing us grief and feeling joy at the sight of our blood. I wish that I could die before you die."

At the tomb of Achilles, Neoptolemus gripped Polyxena tightly with his left hand so she could not run away. He drew his sword with his strong right hand and rested the hilt on the tomb, saying, "Father, do not be angry any longer at the Greeks. Be satisfied with this sacrifice and allow us to return safely home."

Polyxena screamed, and Neoptolemus drove the sword into her throat. She bled much and died quickly.

The Greeks gave Polyxena's body to the Trojan Antenor, whose son Eurymachus had been going to marry her. He buried her by his home, which was near a monument of Ganymede and the temple of Athena. As soon as Polyxena was buried, the winds and waves died down, and the sea was suitable for sailing.

The Greeks sacrificed to the gods, and they feasted and drank. They used goblets of gold and silver that they had taken from the noble palaces of Troy.

After everyone had feasted, Nestor said, "Achilles is no longer angry, Poseidon has calmed the storm at sea, and the time is right to set sail. Let us drag our ships to the sea and go home."

As Nestor had advised, the Greeks dragged their ships to the sea and loaded them with treasure and women taken from Troy and conquered cities that had been allied with Troy.

The gods performed one more marvel before the Greeks set sail. The grieving Hecuba was changed into a dog made out of stone. The Greeks put her on board one of their ships and took her across to the other side of the Hellespont, where they left her at a spot afterward known as Dog's Tomb.

Two Greeks were afraid to set sail immediately. The prophet Calchas worried that the ships would sail into danger when they arrived at the Capherean Rocks at the headland of the southeast end of the island of Euboea. He tried to convince the other Greeks to wait to set sail, but only Amphilochus, who also understood prophecy, stayed with him. Neither Calchas nor Amphilochus would die during their sea journey, but both would go to cities that were not their own.

The Greeks who were immediately setting sail poured wine into the sea as an offering to the gods. Their ships were crowded with armor that they had taken from dead Trojans. Their ships were decorated with garlands signifying victory. The Greeks prayed to the gods for a safe passage home for all and poured wine into the sea as a sacrifice, but their prayers were scattered by the wind.

The Trojan women looked at Troy, from which smoke still rose, as the ships sailed away; they tried to conceal their grief. Some women clasped their knees with their hands; some women held their heads in their hands. Some women held children in their arms. The children, who sucked milk from their mothers' breasts, did not know yet that they were slaves. Their mothers' breasts bore red welts from the scratches the Trojan women had made in their grief. No longer wives, the women did not braid their hair but let it fall loose. On their faces were the traces of dried tears; new tears soon covered up those traces. The Trojan women remembered the prophecies of Cassandra, and they looked at her. Some people sometimes respond to grief and misery in strange ways: Cassandra laughed.

Some Trojans had escaped and run away during the sack of the city. When it was safe for them to do so, they returned and buried the dead. Antenor led the holding of the funerals. The few survivors burned the many corpses of men, women, and children on one funeral pyre.

The Greeks, who rejoiced because of their victory but mourned because of their dead, used oars and sails to leave the Trojan land. They made good time, and it seemed as if all of them would return home safely, but Athena was angry at Little Ajax because he had raped Cassandra in her temple.

When the Greeks sailed close to the island of Euboea, Athena said to Zeus, "Father, mortals no longer respect the gods, who ought to dispense justice. Mortals know that a good man often suffers and that a bad man often rejoices. Because of this, they no longer try to be just — they willingly do evil actions. This is wrong. Evil men ought to be punished. In my own temple, Little Ajax raped Cassandra. This is wrong on many levels. He committed rape. He raped a virgin who was soon to be married. He raped a virgin in a temple as she called on the virgin goddess to whom the temple was dedicated to protect her. Do not stop me as I punish Little Ajax and teach men not to commit rape. I also want to teach them to respect the gods."

Zeus replied, "I will give you all the weapons you need to punish Little Ajax for his rape. Call up a storm against the Greeks. I give you my lightning bolts so you can kill Little Ajax. The Cyclopes made these lightning bolts for me."

Athena put on a breastplate on which was displayed the head of Medusa with its writhing, fire-breathing snakes, she picked up her father's thunderbolts, and she sent a message to Aeolus, the god of the winds, to cause a storm at sea to raise huge waves and sink ships. Iris took Athena's message to Aeolus, who was with his wife and their twelve children. He listened to Iris, and then he used his trident to strike the side of the mountain in which was a cave that housed the winds. Aeolus' trident broke a hole in the mountain, and the winds rushed out. Poseidon helped Athena by sending waves to batter the ships.

The waves raised the ships high and then dropped them low as if they were falling from a mountain into an abyss in which sand boiled up from the bottom of the sea.

The winds of Aeolus pummeled the ships. Zeus' lightning bolts terrified the Greeks. Athena laughed.

The Greeks could do little or nothing to save themselves. They could not row or manage their sails. Their pilots could not steer their ships. Ships collided and crushed Greek men and Trojan women and children. Many fell into the sea and drowned. Some held onto pieces of oars and other wreckage and hoped to survive.

Athena threw a lightning bolt that shattered the ship of Little Ajax and scattered its pieces across the waves. Many Trojan women were happy to die even if it meant the death of their children, whom they held in their arms. Some Trojan women tightly gripped Greeks so that they could not swim; the Trojan women were eager to make Greeks die with them.

Little Ajax grabbed onto a piece of wreckage and stayed afloat; he was strong like a Titan. The waves lifted him and then let him drop. The gods marveled at his ability to stay alive in the storming sea.

Athena knew that he would die, and she wanted him to suffer before he died. Little Ajax, however, did not know that he would die. He boasted that he would live even if all the Olympian gods were against him.

Little Ajax grabbed onto a rock, and struggled to hold on to it as his hands grew bloody, but Poseidon broke the rock that Little Ajax was holding onto and Little Ajax fell into the sea. Even then, he could have escaped death, but Poseidon sent the rock after Little Ajax to land on top of him and carry him to the bottom of the sea and bury him. Athena had once lifted the island of Sicily and covered the giant Enceladus with it; Poseidon now covered Little Ajax with a huge rock.

The Greek ships were either sunk or badly damaged by the storm. Heavy rain fell. One Greek said, "In the days of Deucalion, storms such as this raged. He had sacrificed a boy to Zeus, who was disgusted by such a sacrifice, and Zeus sent storms to flood the world."

Many corpses floated in the sea, and many corpses were cast onto the nearby land. This made Nauplius, the son of Poseidon and the father of Palamedes, happy. Odysseus had not wanted to go to Troy, and so had feigned madness, but Palamedes discovered the fakery and so Odysseus had to go to war. Odysseus never forgave Palamedes for that, and in revenge, according to rumor, he got Palamedes killed. Nauplius wanted justice for his son's death, but the Greeks refused to give him justice, and so Nauplius prayed for the destruction of many Greeks and their ships. Poseidon granted that prayer.

Nauplius personally caused the death of many Greeks. On a dangerous shore, he held up a flaming torch. The Greeks thought that it was a signal directing them to a safe harbor, so they sailed toward the torch, and their ships and their bodies broke on the rocks of a reef.

Athena was happy in the destruction of ships and lives, but she respected Odysseus and she mourned because she knew that he was fated to suffer from the future anger of Poseidon at him.

Poseidon, with the help of Zeus and Apollo, destroyed the defensive fortifications the Greeks had built at Troy. Floods and an earthquake swept away the Greeks' defensive wall and filled in their trench. After this destruction, only sand could still be seen.

The storm eventually ended, as all things do, and the surviving Greeks continued their sea voyages and tried to reach their homes, bringing their slaves with them.

Conclusion

I am aware of three English translations of Quintus of Smyrna's epic poem, which is often called the *Posthomerica*, or *After Homer*, although *After Homer's Iliad* would be a better title:

Quintus of Smyrna. *The Trojan Epic: Posthomerica*. Translated and edited by Alan James. Baltimore and London: The Johns Hopkins Press, 2004.

Quintus of Smyrna. *The War at Troy: What Homer Didn't Tell*. Trans. Frederick M. Combellack. Norman, Oklahoma: University of Oklahoma Press, 1968.

Quintus Smyrnaeus. *The Fall of Troy*. Trans. Arthur S. Way. Cambridge, Massachusetts, and London, England: Harvard University Press, 2000. First published 1913.

If you are interested in reading the real thing now that you have read this retelling, I recommend that you read the translation by Alan James. I like the translation by Frederick M. Combellack, but it is in prose, and you have already read this prose retelling. Since Quintus of Smyrna wrote an epic poem, it is a good idea to read a translation that keeps it as poetry. The translation by Arthur S. Way is good, but it is old and uses some old-fashioned language. I very much like the translation by Alan James, and it has the advantage of using better sources than were available to the other two translators.

Appendix A: Background Information

Roman Gods and Goddesses

The Greek gods and goddesses have Roman equivalents. The Greek name is followed by the Roman name:

Aphrodite: Venus

Apollo: Apollo (same name)

Ares: Mars

Artemis: Diana

Athena: Minerva

Hades: Pluto

Hephaestus: Vulcan

Hera: Juno

Hermes: Mercury

Poseidon: Neptune

Zeus: Jupiter

Note: The Romans referred to Odysseus as Ulysses.

- **What are the *Iliad* and the *Odyssey*?**

The *Iliad* and the *Odyssey* are epic poems that have been created by Homer. Here are two definitions of "epic poem":

- a long narrative poem about the adventures of [a] hero or the gods, presenting an encyclopedic portrait of the culture in which it is composed.

Source: <teacherweb.com/NC/OrangeHighSchool/ MrMitchCox/HandyLiteraryandAnglo-SaxonTerms.doc[1]>

- a long narrative poem telling of a hero's deeds.

Source: <wordnet.princeton.edu/perl/webwn[2]>

---

1. http://www.google.com/url?sa=X&start=0&oi=define&q=http://teacherweb.com/NC/ OrangeHighSchool/MrMitchCox/HandyLiteraryandAnglo- SaxonTerms.doc&usg=AFQjCNGaBbztLE3YBGtw0kVDdkCOHVVn-Q

The *Iliad* tells the story of one incident that lasted a few weeks during the last year of the Trojan War: a quarrel between Achilles, the mightiest of the Greek (Achaean) warriors, and Agamemnon, leader of the Greek armies against Troy. Both Achilles and Agamemnon are kings of their own lands, but Agamemnon is the leader among the many kings fighting the Trojans and the Trojan allies. The quarrel between Achilles and Agamemnon has devastating consequences.

• **What is the mythic background of the *Iliad* and the *Odyssey*?**

The mythic background of the *Iliad* and the *Odyssey* consists of the Trojan War myth and myths about the Greek gods and goddesses.

• **For what other works did this mythic background provide narrative material?**

The Trojan War myth provided material for many other epic poems, both Greek and Roman, some of which have survived, and for many plays, including both tragedies and comedies, by both Greek and Roman authors. The Trojan War myth is one of the most important myths in the world.

During Roman times, the Trojan War myth provided material for Virgil's great epic poem the *Aeneid*, which tells the story of Aeneas and how he survived the fall of Troy and came to Italy to found (establish) the Roman people. He and his Italian wife, Lavinia, became important ancestors of the Romans. Later, Dante used material from the Trojan War myth and its aftermath in his *Divine Comedy*. Material from the Trojan War myth has appeared in opera and in drama. Of course, James Joyce uses this material in his novel *Ulysses*.

• **Why is it important to understand the Trojan War myth when reading the *Iliad* and the *Odyssey*?**

Homer's audience knew the story of the Trojan War. How did Homer's audience get its understanding of the Trojan War? Partly through stories told by their parents and grandparents. As they were growing up, they heard tales about the myth. Therefore, Homer assumes a lot of knowledge in his audience. Homer does not tell the story of the Trojan Horse; he assumes that his audience already knows the story. Homer does not tell the story of the Trojan War; he assumes that his audience already knows the story. Without a knowledge of the

---

2. http://www.google.com/url?sa=X&start=1&oi=define&q=http://wordnet.princeton.edu/perl/

webwn%3Fs%3Depic+poem&usg=AFQjCNEd1O6O1iYkAZOlEWZIuFs9Lf3-5w

Trojan War, the audience will not be able to appreciate fully the *Iliad* and the *Odyssey*.

• What is the *Iliad* about?

The *Iliad* tells the story of the quarrel between Achilles and Agamemnon. Following the quarrel, Achilles (the mightiest Greek warrior) withdraws from the fighting, which allows the Trojans to be triumphant in battle for a while. The *Iliad* tells about Achilles' anger and how he finally lets go of his anger.

• What is the *Odyssey* about?

The *Odyssey* is about a different Greek hero in the Trojan War: Odysseus, whose Roman name is Ulysses. Following the ten years that the Trojan War lasted, Odysseus returns to his home island of Ithaca, where he is king. It takes him ten years to return home because of his adventures and mishaps. Much of that time he spends in captivity. When he finally returns home, he discovers that suitors are courting his wife, Penelope, who has remained faithful to him and who wants nothing to do with the suitors, who are rude and arrogant and who feast on Odysseus' cattle and drink his wine as they party all day. In addition, Telemachus, Odysseus' son, has found it hard to grow up without a strong father-figure in his life. The *Odyssey* tells the story of how Odysseus returns home to Ithaca and reestablishes himself in his own palace.

• What does *nostos* mean?

Nostos means "Homecoming" or "Return." This is important to know because this is the theme of the *Odyssey*. In this epic poem, we read about the homecoming of Odysseus to Ithaca, the island where he is king. Odysseus has been away from Ithaca for 20 years. He spent ten years fighting in the Trojan War, and it took him an additional ten years to return to Ithaca, after having lost all his ships and men.

The great theme of the *Iliad* is *kleos*, which means imperishable glory or the reputation that lives on after one has died if one has accomplished great deeds during one's battles. The great theme of the *Odyssey* is *nostos*.

The *Iliad* is concerned with the Trojan War, and the *Odyssey* is concerned with the aftermath of the Trojan War.

• What is the *Aeneid* about?

The *Aeneid* is a Roman epic poem by Virgil that tells the story of Aeneas, a Trojan prince who survived the fall of Troy and led other survivors to Italy. His adventures parallel the adventures of Odysseus on his return to Ithaca. In fact, they visit many of the same places, including the island of the Cyclopes. One of Aeneas' most notable characteristics is his *pietas*, his respect for things for which respect is due, including the gods, his family, and his destiny. His destiny is to found the Roman people, which is different from founding Rome, which was founded long after his death. Aeneas journeyed to Carthage, where he had an affair with Dido, the Carthaginian queen. Because of his destiny, he left her and went to Italy. Dido committed suicide, and Aeneas fought a war to establish himself in Italy. After killing Turnus, the leader of the armies facing him, Aeneas married the Italian princess Lavinia, and they became important ancestors of the Roman people.

• What is the basic story of the Trojan War?

Paris, Prince of Troy, visits Menelaus, King of Sparta, and then Paris runs off with Menelaus' wife, Helen, who of course becomes known as Helen of Troy. This is a major insult to Menelaus and his family, so he and his elder brother, Agamemnon, lead an army against Troy to get Helen (and reparations) back. The war drags on for ten years, and the greatest Greek warrior is Achilles, while the greatest Trojan warrior is Hector, Paris' eldest brother. Eventually, Hector is killed by Achilles, who is then killed by Paris, who is then killed by Philoctetes. Finally, Odysseus comes up with the idea of the Trojan Horse, which ends the Trojan War.

That is a brief retelling of the Trojan War, but many, many myths grew up around the war, making it a richly detailed myth.

• Does Homer allude to all of the details of the Trojan War?

Homer does not allude to all the details of the Trojan War. For example, one myth states that Achilles was invincible except for his heel. According to this myth, his mother, the goddess Thetis, knew that Achilles was fated to die in the Trojan War; therefore, to protect him, she dipped him into a pool of water that was supposed to make him invulnerable. To do that, she held him by his heel. Because she was holding him by his heel, the water did not touch it and so that part of Achilles' body remained vulnerable.

Homer never alludes to this myth; in fact, this myth plays no role whatsoever in Homer's epic poems. Achilles is not invulnerable. If he were, he could fight in battle naked, as long as he wore an iron boot over his vulnerable heel. In Homer, Achilles is vulnerable to weapons, and he knows it. At one point, he would like to join the fighting, but he cannot, because he has no armor. No one who reads the *Iliad* should think that Achilles is invulnerable except for his heel.

Myth changes and develops over time, and it is possible that Homer had no knowledge of this myth because it had not been created yet. Or it is possible that Homer knew of this myth but ignored it because he had his own points to make in his epic poem.

Another myth that may or may not be alluded to is the Judgment of Paris. It may be alluded to in a couple of places in the *Iliad*, but scholars disagree about this.

• Who is Achilles, and what is unusual about his mother, Thetis?

Achilles, of course, is the foremost warrior of the Greeks during the Trojan War. His mother, Thetis, is unusual in that she is a goddess. The Greeks' religion was different from many modern religions in that the Greeks were polytheistic (believing in many gods) rather than monotheistic (believing in one god). In addition, the gods and human beings could mate. Achilles is unusual in that he had an immortal goddess as his mother and a mortal man, Peleus, as his father. Achilles, of course, is unusual in many ways. Another way in which he is unusual is that he and Thetis have long talks together. Often, the gods either ignore their mortal offspring or choose not to reveal themselves to them. For example, Aeneas' goddess mother is Aphrodite (Roman name: Venus). Although Aphrodite does save Aeneas' life or help him on occasion, the two do not have long talks together the way that Achilles and Thetis do.

• What prophecy was made about Thetis' male offspring?

The prophecy about Thetis' male offspring was that he would be a greater man than his father. This is something that would make most human fathers happy. (One exception would be Pap, in Mark Twain's *Adventures of Huckleberry Finn*. Pap does not want Huck, his son, to learn to read or write or to get an education or to live better than Pap does.)

• Who is Zeus, and what does he decide to do as a result of this prophecy?

Zeus is a horny god who sleeps with many goddesses and many human beings. Normally, he would lust after Thetis, but once he hears the prophecy, he does not want to sleep with Thetis. For one thing, the gods are potent, and when they mate they have children. Zeus overthrew his own father, and Zeus does not want Thetis to give birth to a greater man than he is because his son will overthrow him. Therefore, Zeus wants to get Thetis married off to someone else. In this case, a marriage to a human being for Thetis would suit Zeus just fine. A human son may be greater than his father, but he is still not going to be as great as a god, and so Zeus will be safe if Thetis gives birth to a human son.

• Who is Peleus?

Peleus is the human man who marries Thetis and who fathers Achilles. At the time of the *Iliad*, Peleus is an old man and Thetis has not lived with him for a long time.

• Why is Eris, Goddess of Discord, not invited to the wedding feast of Peleus and Thetis?

Obviously, you do not want discord at a wedding, and therefore, Eris, Goddess of Discord, is not invited to the wedding feast of Peleus and Thetis. Even though Eris is not invited to the wedding feast, she shows up anyway.

• Eris, Goddess of Discord, throws an apple on a table at the wedding feast. What is inscribed on the apple?

Inscribed on the apple is the phrase "For the fairest," written in Greek, of course. Because Greek is a language that indicates masculine and feminine in certain words, and since "fairest" has a feminine ending, the apple is really inscribed "for the fairest female."

• Hera, Athena, and Aphrodite each claim the apple. Who are they?

Three goddesses claim the apple, meaning that each of the three goddesses thinks that she is the fairest, or most beautiful.

Hera

Hera is the wife of Zeus, and she is a jealous wife. Zeus has many affairs with both immortal goddesses and mortal women, and Hera is jealous because of these affairs. Zeus would like to keep on her good side.

Athena

Athena is the goddess of wisdom. She becomes the patron goddess of Athens. Athena especially likes Odysseus, as we see especially in the *Odyssey*. Athena is a favorite of Zeus, her father. Zeus would like to keep on her good side.

Aphrodite

Aphrodite is the goddess of sexual passion. She can make Zeus fall in love against his will. Zeus would like to keep on her good side.

• Why doesn't Zeus want to judge the goddesses' beauty contest?

Zeus is not a fool. He knows that if he judges the goddesses' beauty contest, he will make two enemies. The two goddesses whom Zeus does not choose as the fairest will hate him and likely make trouble for him.

Please note that the Greek gods and goddesses are not omnibenevolent. Frequently, they are quarrelsome and petty.

By the way, Athens, Ohio, lawyer Thomas Hodson once judged a beauty contest featuring 25 cute child contestants. He was running in an election to choose the municipal court judge, and he thought that judging the contest would be a good way to win votes. Very quickly, he decided never to judge a children's beauty contest again. He figured out that he had won two votes — the votes of the parents of the child who won the contest. Unfortunately, he also figured out that he had lost 48 votes — the votes of the parents of the children who lost.

• Who is Paris, and what is the Judgment of Paris?

Paris is a prince of Troy, and Zeus allows him to judge the three goddesses' beauty contest. Paris is not as intelligent as Zeus, or he would try to find a way out of judging the beauty contest.

• Each of the goddesses offers Paris a bribe if he will choose her. What are the bribes?

Hera

Hera offers Paris political power: several cities he can rule.

Athena

Athena offers Paris prowess in battle. Paris can become a mighty and feared warrior.

Aphrodite

Aphrodite offers Paris the most beautiful woman in the world to be his wife.

• Which goddess does Paris choose?

Paris chooses Aphrodite, who offered him the most beautiful woman in the world to be his wife.

This is not what a Homeric warrior would normally choose. A person such as Achilles would choose to be an even greater warrior, if that is possible.

A person such as Agamemnon is likely to choose more cities to rule.

When Paris chooses the most beautiful woman in the world to be his wife, we are not meant to think that he made a good decision. Paris is not a likable character.

• As a result of Aphrodite's bribe, Paris abducts Helen. Why?

Aphrodite promised Paris the most beautiful woman to be his wife. As it happens, that woman is Helen. Therefore, Paris abducts Helen, with Aphrodite's approval.

Did Helen go with Paris willingly? The answer to this question is ambiguous, and ancient authorities varied in how they answered this question.

• To whom is Helen already married?

Helen is already married to Menelaus, the King of Sparta. Paris visits Menelaus, and when he leaves, he carries off both a lot of Menelaus' treasure and Menelaus' wife, Helen. Obviously, this is not the way that one ought to treat one's host.

• Who are Agamemnon and Menelaus?

Agamemnon and Menelaus are the sons of Atreus. They are brothers, and Agamemnon, the king of Mycenae, is the older brother and the brother who rules a greater land, as seen by the number of ships the two kings bring to the Trojan War. Menelaus brings 60 ships. Agamemnon brings 100 ships.

• Who is responsible for leading the expedition to recover Helen?

Agamemnon is the older brother, so he is the leader of the Greek troops in the Trojan War.

• Why do the winds blow against the Greek ships?

When the Greek ships are gathered together and are ready to set sail against Troy, a wind blows in the wrong direction for them to sail. The goddess Artemis (Roman name: Diana) is angry at the Greeks because she knows that the result of the Trojan War will be lots of death, not just of warriors, but also of women and children. This is true of all wars, and it is a lesson that human beings forget after each war and relearn in the next war.

• Why does Artemis demand a human sacrifice?

Artemis knows that Agamemnon's warriors will cause much death of children, so she makes him sacrifice one of his daughters so that he will suffer what he will make other parents suffer.

• Who does Agamemnon sacrifice?

Agamemnon sacrifices his daughter Iphigeneia. This is a religious sacrifice of a human life to appease the goddess Artemis.

• What do Menelaus and Agamemnon do?

After the sacrifice of Iphigenia, Agamemnon and Menelaus set sail with all the Greek ships for Troy. They land, then they engage in warfare.

• Who are Achilles and Hector?

Achilles is the foremost Greek warrior, while Hector is the foremost Trojan warrior. Both warriors are deserving of great respect.

• Does Homer assume that Achilles is invulnerable?

Absolutely not. Achilles needs armor to go out on the battlefield and fight.

• What happens to Hector and Achilles?

Hector kills Achilles' best friend, Patroclus, in battle. Angry, Achilles kills Hector.

• What is the story of the Trojan Horse?

Odysseus, a great strategist, thought up the idea of the Trojan Horse. Epeus built it.

The Greeks build a giant wooden horse, which is hollow and filled with Greek warriors, and then they pretend to abandon the war and to sail away from Troy. Actually, Agamemnon sails behind an island so that the Trojans cannot see the Greek ships. The Greeks also leave behind a lying Greek named Sinon, who tells the Trojans about a supposed prophecy that if the Trojans take the Trojan Horse inside their city, then Troy will never fall. The Trojans do that, and at night the Greeks come out of the Trojan Horse, make their way to the city gates and open them. Outside the city gates are the Greek troops led by Agamemnon, who have returned to the Trojan plain. The Greek warriors rush inside the city and sack it.

Virgil's *Aeneid* has the fullest surviving ancient account of the Trojan Horse. Of course, he tells the story from the Trojan point of view. If Homer had written the story of the Trojan Horse, he would have told it from the Greek point of view. For the Greeks, the Trojan War ended in a great victory. For the Trojans, the Trojan War ended in a great disaster.

• Which outrages do the Greeks commit during the sack of Troy?

The Greeks committed many outrages during the sack of Troy:

Killing of King Priam

King Priam is killed by Achilles' son, Neoptolemus, aka Pyrrhus, at the altar of Zeus. This is an outrage because anyone who is at the altar of a god is under the protection of that god. When Neoptolemus kills Priam, an old man (and old people are respected in Homeric culture), Neoptolemus disrespects the god Zeus.

Killing of Hector's Young Son

Hector's son is murdered. Hector's son is a very small child who is murdered by being hurled from the top of a high wall of Troy. Even during wartime, children ought not to be murdered, so this is another outrage.

Rape of Cassandra

Cassandra is raped by Little Ajax even though she is under Athena's protection. Cassandra is raped in a temple devoted to Athena. This is showing major disrespect to Athena. Again, the Greeks are doing things that ought not to be done, even during wartime.

Sacrifice of Polyxena

The Greeks sacrificed Priam's young daughter Polyxena. The Trojan War begins and ends with a human sacrifice of the life of a young girl. This is yet another outrage.

- **How do the gods react to these outrages?**

The gods and goddesses make things difficult for the Greeks on their way home to Greece.

- **What happens to the Greeks after the fall of Troy?**

Nestor is a wise, pious, old man who did not commit any outrages. He makes it home quickly.

Apparently, Odysseus' patron goddess, Athena, is angry at all of the Greeks, because she does not help him on his journey home until ten years have passed.

Little Ajax, who raped Cassandra, drowns on his way home.

Agamemnon returns home to a world of trouble. His wife, Clytemnestra, has taken a lover during his ten-year absence, and she murders Agamemnon.

Menelaus is reunited with Helen, but their ship is driven off course, and it takes them years to return home to Sparta.

- **What happens to Aeneas?**

Aeneas fights bravely, and he witnesses such things as the death of Priam, King of Troy; however, when he realizes that Troy is lost, he returns to his family to try to save them. He carries his father on his back, and he leads his young son by the hand, but although he saves them by leading them out of Troy, his wife, who is following behind him, is lost in the battle.

Aeneas becomes the leader of the Trojan survivors, and he leads them to Italy, where they become the founders of the Roman people.

• **Who were the Roman people?**

The Romans had one of the greatest empires of the world.

• **In the Homeric epics, are human beings responsible for their actions?**

Yes, human beings are responsible for their actions in the Homeric epics.

• **Despite Aphrodite, is Paris responsible for his actions?**

Of course, Aphrodite promised Paris the most beautiful woman in the world to be his wife if Paris chose her as the fairest of the three goddesses who wanted the golden apple. However, Paris is responsible for his actions when he runs away with Helen, the lawful wife of Menelaus. Paris could have declined to run away with Helen.

• **Is Agamemnon responsible for his actions?**

Artemis required the sacrifice of Agamemnon's daughter before the winds would blow the Greek ships to Troy, but Agamemnon is still responsible for his actions. He could have declined to sacrifice his daughter, and he could have given up the war.

• **What happens to humans who do impious acts?**

Humans who do impious acts are punished for their impious acts.

• **What is the Greek concept of fate?**

The Greeks believe in fate. We are fated to die at a certain time, although we do not know when we will die.

In addition, people may be fated to do certain things in their lives. For example, Oedipus is fated to kill his father and to marry his mother.

Similarly, certain events are fated to happen. For example, Troy is fated to be conquered in the Trojan War.

• **Do the *Iliad* and the *Odyssey* tell the entire story of the Trojan War?**

No, they tell only a small part of the story. The *Iliad* tells the story of an event that occurred in a few weeks of the beginning of the final year of the Trojan War. The story of the Trojan War is not fully told in either epic poem. Neither is the story of the Trojan Horse, although knowledge of it is essential for understanding the *Iliad,* and although the Trojan Horse is talked about briefly in the *Odyssey.*

- **What happened the first time the author of this retelling read the *Iliad*?**

I read the *Iliad* for the first time the summer before I started college. It was my way of preparing myself to be educated. As I got near the end of the *Iliad*, I started wondering, "Where is the Trojan Horse?" When I got to the end of the *Iliad*, I was very surprised that Troy had not yet fallen.

- **Did other epics exist?**

Yes, other epics did exist, and we do have some Roman epics that were written much later than the *Iliad* and the *Odyssey*, of course. The ancient Greek epics from the time of Homer have not survived. Fortunately, we know from ancient commentators that we have the really good epic poems. The epics that have been lost were not as good as the *Iliad* and the *Odyssey*.

- **What do the Homeric epics assume?**

The Homeric epics assume that you know the mythic background, which is why I have written about it here.

- **What is the society described in the Homeric epics like?**

Homeric society is very different from our society; it is patriarchal, slave-holding, monarchical, and polytheistic:

Patriarchal

This is a society in which the men have the power. Of course, the goddesses are a special case and are more powerful than human men. However, even in the world of gods and goddesses, the gods have more power. The king of the gods is Zeus, a male. Often, contemporary USAmerican society is thought of as patriarchal. I won't deny that, but the ancient Greek society was much more patriarchal than contemporary USAmerican society.

Slave-Holding

Slaves exist in the *Iliad* and the *Odyssey*. In the *Iliad*, women are spoils of war, and young, pretty women become sex-slaves to the warriors who have killed their husbands. In the *Odyssey*, slaves are servants in the palace and on the farm. Slavery is taken for granted in the Homeric epics.

Monarchical

Kings exist in the *Iliad* and the *Odyssey*. Agamemnon is a king, Menelaus is a king, Achilles is a king, and Odysseus is a king.

Polytheistic

As we have seen, the ancient Greeks and Romans believed in many gods with a small g. We moderns tend to believe or to disbelieve in one God with a capital G.

• What do we mean by *theos*?

The Greek word *theos* (THAY os) is usually translated as "god" with a small g. Yes, this is a good translation of the word, but we modern readers can be misled by it because of our familiarity with the word "God" with a capital G.

• Are the gods personified forces of nature?

Originally, the gods seem to have been personified forces of nature. They are more than that in the Homeric epics, but they are still in part personified forces of nature.

One example is that Zeus is the god of the sky and lightning. Of course, in the *Iliad* Zeus is much more than merely the god of the sky and lightning. Maybe that is how belief in Zeus arose, but Zeus became much more than that.

Another example is that Poseidon is the god of the sea.

Another example is that Ares is war. (Here we have an embodiment of human culture rather than an embodiment of a force of nature.) In the *Iliad*, Zeus says that Ares is hated. He is hated because he is war.

Another example is that Aphrodite is sexual passion. She is the personification of sexual passion. We can say that she inflicts sexual passion on other people, but in addition, she is sexual passion. This is not just a way of speaking. Someone may say, "Aphrodite filled me with lust"; in other words, Aphrodite is a way of explaining human emotion. However, in the Homeric epics, Aphrodite is more than a way of explaining human emotion. In Book 3 of Homer's *Iliad*, Aphrodite forces Helen to go to bed with Paris. She threatens Helen, and she takes Helen to Paris' bedroom.

• Are the gods anthropomorphic?

These gods are anthropomorphic. They have human form, with some differences. The gods and goddesses are larger and better looking and stronger than human beings. However, they look like human beings, and they speak the language of human beings. They also eat, drink, and have sex like human beings. They also feel the human emotions of jealousy (Hera is jealous of Zeus' love affairs), passion (Zeus sleeps with many, many females, both mortal and immortal), anger (Ares becomes angry when he is wounded by Diomedes in battle), and grief (Zeus grieves because his son Sarpedon is fated to die).

• Are the gods omnibenevolent, omniscient, or omnipotent?

The Homeric gods are not omnibenevolent, omniscient, or omnipotent.

Not Omnibenevolent

Clearly, the gods are not omnibenevolent. They are not all-good; they are not even just. Some of the gods are rapists. Hera is very capable of exacting vengeance on innocent people. The gods are very dangerous, and they can do bad things to human beings. One example is the myth of Actaeon. He was out hunting with his dogs, and he saw the goddess Artemis bathing naked. He did not mean to see her naked, but she exacts vengeance anyway. She turns him into a stag, and he is run down and killed by his own dogs. He suffers horribly because his mind is still human although his body is that of a male deer.

Not Omniscient

In addition, the gods are not omniscient. We see this in the *Odyssey*. Athena has been wanting to help Odysseus, but she does not want to anger Poseidon, who is opposed to Odysseus. Therefore, Athena waits until Poseidon's attention is turned elsewhere, and then she helps Odysseus. Another example is that when Hera seduces Zeus in the *Iliad*, he does not know that she is tricking him. Hera wants to seduce Zeus so that he will go to sleep, and the Achaeans will be triumphant in the battle. If Zeus were omniscient, he would have known that she was tricking him. Of course, the gods do know a lot. For example, they know a human being's fate. In addition, the gods hear prayers addressed to them.

Not Omnipotent

The gods are very powerful, but they are not omnipotent. The gods can change their shape. They can take the shape of a bird or of a particular human being. The gods can travel very quickly. Poseidon can cause earthquakes, and Zeus can cause lightning. The gods cannot go back on their inviolable oaths. For example: When Alcmene was about to give birth to Heracles, Zeus announced that on a certain day a boy would be born who was both a descendant of Perseus, an ancient hero, and who would rule over the city of Mycenae, which later Agamemnon ruled. Unfortunately, this news allowed Hera to interfere. Hera is the goddess of childbirth, and she was able to delay the birth of Heracles. She also was able to speed up the birth of Eurystheus, who was a descendant of Perseus. By doing this, Hera brought it about that Eurystheus, not Heracles, ruled Mycenae. Hera made sure that Eurystheus was born on that day, and not Heracles. After all, Zeus had sworn an inviolable oath that a descendant of Perseus born on that day would rule Mycenae, and the gods, including Zeus, cannot go back on their inviolable oaths.

- **What does *xenia* mean?**

Xenia is often defined as the guest-host relationship. English does not have a word like *xenia*, although "hospitality" is sometimes used as a translation of *xenia*. However, "hospitality" is too weak a word for what the ancient Greeks meant. The word *xenia* carries with it an obligation to the gods. Zeus is the god of *xenia*, and when people abuse their sacred duty of *xenia*, they are disrespecting Zeus.

- **In which way is *xenia* a reciprocal relationship?**

Xenia is a reciprocal relationship between guest and host in both the *Odyssey* and the *Iliad*.

Xenia is a reciprocal relationship between two *xenoi*. (*Xenoi* is the plural; *xenos* is the singular.)

Xenos can mean five different things, depending on the context: guest, host, stranger, friend, and foreigner.

- **Which meanings does *xenos* have?**

In ancient Greece, no hotels or motels existed. If you were traveling and you arrived at a town in the evening, you would look for hospitality at a home. In such a case, you and your host would be *xenoi*.

In this case, you would be a guest, a stranger, and a foreigner. You would be a guest in this home. Because your host doesn't know you, you would be a stranger. Because you aren't from this town, you would be a foreigner.

Of course, your host would be a host.

In addition, you and your host would be friends. You would not be friends in the sense that you have known and liked each other for a long time. You would be friends because you have participated in the guest-host relationship.

By the way, *xenia* is a root word of *xenophobia*, or fear of strangers.

In addition, modern Greece has the tradition today of *xenophilia*, or of showing hospitality to tourists.

- **Which safeguards protect against the violation of *xenia*?**

There can be a lot of danger in such a relationship. What would happen if either the guest or the host were a robber and a killer? Bad things.

Therefore, there needs to be some kind of safeguard in place. The host must not murder his guest. The guest must not murder his host.

Sinbad's Poverty Tour: Early in Sinbad the comedian's career, he knew that he needed to have more experience if he wanted to be a stand-up comedian. Therefore, he went out on what he called his Poverty Tour. He simply loaded up the truck of his car with some tools and clothing, drove to a city, and looked for places where he could do his act. He would tell the owner of the club that he wouldn't charge him or her anything and he would pass the hat around for tips after his act. This was OK with the owners, as it saved them money. Of course, Sinbad didn't make much money that way, and he often slept in his car. To solve that problem, when he did his act for the last time at night, he would ask the audience if someone would let him sleep on their couch. Of course, Sinbad is a big guy and he can take care of himself. He would look over the prospective host, and if he looked OK, he would go home with him and sleep on the couch. If the prospective host looked dangerous, Sinbad would say that he was going to get his car, but he would drive off. Sinbad was a good guest, by the way. In his day job, he had done plumbing and carpentry work. He would unobtrusively look around his host's apartment, find something that needed fixed, and then he would say, "Hey, I've got my tools in my car. Let me fix that for you." Sinbad said that he always left the apartments where he stayed as a guest in better shape than they were when he arrived.

The ancient Greeks did have a safeguard for *xenia*: Zeus *Xenios*, which means Zeus, the god of *xenia*. Anyone who does not follow the rules of *xenia* is not doing the will of Zeus. This offends Zeus, and eventually the offender will pay for his transgression.

• In which way was the cause of the Trojan War a violation of *xenia*?

Of course, the Trojan War began because of a violation of *xenia*. The Trojan Paris was a guest of Menelaus, King of Sparta. When you are a guest, you aren't supposed to run away with your host's wife and much of his treasure. We know what happened to Troy as a result of this transgression of *xenia*: the Greeks conquered Troy. As you can see, *xenia* is important in the *Odyssey*, but it is important also in the *Iliad*.

• An example of bad *xenia*.

How evil were the people of Sodom? When a stranger arrived in their city, each citizen would give him a piece of gold that had been marked with the name of the giver. The stranger would be grateful, of course, to receive the gold, but he would quickly find that he was unable to spend it. Each time he would attempt to buy food, the shop owners would refuse to sell it to him. In addition, the stranger found that he was unable to leave the city — the guards would not allow him to pass through the gates. Therefore, the stranger — despite his pile of gold coins — would slowly starve to death. When the stranger had starved to death, the citizens would come by the pile of gold coins, pick up the coin with their name marked on it and wait to starve to death another stranger.

Appendix B: About the Author

It was a dark and stormy night. Suddenly a cry rang out, and on a hot summer night in 1954, Josephine, wife of Carl Bruce, gave birth to a boy — me. Unfortunately, this young married couple allowed Reuben Saturday, Josephine's brother, to name their first-born. Reuben, aka "The Joker," decided that Bruce was a nice name, so he decided to name me Bruce Bruce. I have gone by my middle name — David — ever since.

Being named Bruce David Bruce hasn't been all bad. Bank tellers remember me very quickly, so I don't often have to show an ID. It can be fun in charades, also. When I was a counselor as a teenager at Camp Echoing Hills in Warsaw, Ohio, a fellow counselor gave the signs for "sounds like" and "two words," then she pointed to a bruise on her leg twice. Bruise Bruise? Oh yeah, Bruce Bruce is the answer!

Uncle Reuben, by the way, gave me a haircut when I was in kindergarten. He cut my hair short and shaved a small bald spot on the back of my head. My mother wouldn't let me go to school until the bald spot grew out again.

Of all my brothers and sisters (six in all), I am the only transplant to Athens, Ohio. I was born in Newark, Ohio, and have lived all around Southeastern Ohio. However, I moved to Athens to go to Ohio University and have never left.

At Ohio U, I never could make up my mind whether to major in English or Philosophy, so I got a bachelor's degree with a double major in both areas, then I added a Master of Arts degree in English and a Master of Arts degree in Philosophy. Yes, I have my MAMA degree.

Currently, and for a long time to come (I eat fruits and veggies), I am spending my retirement writing books such as Nadia Comaneci: Perfect 10, *The Funniest People in Dance*, *Homer's Iliad: A Retelling in Prose*, and William Shakespeare's *Othello: A Retelling in Prose*.

By the way, my sister Brenda Kennedy writes romances such as *A New Beginning* and *Shattered Dreams*.

Appendix C: Some Books by David Bruce

Retellings of a Classic Work of Literature

Arden of Faversham: *A Retelling*

Ben Jonson's The Alchemist: *A Retelling*

Ben Jonson's The Arraignment, or Poetaster: *A Retelling*

Ben Jonson's Bartholomew Fair: *A Retelling*

Ben Jonson's The Case is Altered: *A Retelling*

Ben Jonson's Catiline's Conspiracy: *A Retelling*

Ben Jonson's The Devil is an Ass: *A Retelling*

Ben Jonson's Epicene: *A Retelling*

Ben Jonson's Every Man in His Humor: *A Retelling*

Ben Jonson's Every Man Out of His Humor: *A Retelling*

Ben Jonson's The Fountain of Self-Love, or Cynthia's Revels: *A Retelling*

Ben Jonson's The Magnetic Lady, or Humors Reconciled: *A Retelling*

Ben Jonson's The New Inn, or The Light Heart: *A Retelling*

Ben Jonson's Sejanus' Fall: *A Retelling*

Ben Jonson's The Staple of News: *A Retelling*

Ben Jonson's A Tale of a Tub: *A Retelling*

Ben Jonson's Volpone, or the Fox: *A Retelling*

Christopher Marlowe's Complete Plays: Retellings

Christopher Marlowe's Dido, Queen of Carthage: *A Retelling*

Christopher Marlowe's Doctor Faustus: *Retellings of the 1604 A-Text and of the 1616 B-Text*

Christopher Marlowe's Edward II: *A Retelling*

Christopher Marlowe's The Massacre at Paris: *A Retelling*

Christopher Marlowe's The Rich Jew of Malta: *A Retelling*

Christopher Marlowe's Tamburlaine, Parts 1 and 2: *Retellings*

Dante's Divine Comedy: *A Retelling in Prose*

Dante's Inferno: *A Retelling in Prose*

Dante's Purgatory: *A Retelling in Prose*

Dante's Paradise: *A Retelling in Prose*

The Famous Victories of Henry V: *A Retelling*

From the Iliad *to the* Odyssey: *A Retelling in Prose of Quintus of Smyrna's* Posthomerica

George Chapman, Ben Jonson, and John Marston's Eastward Ho! *A Retelling*

George Peele's The Arraignment of Paris: *A Retelling*

George Peele's The Battle of Alcazar: *A Retelling*

George's Peele's David and Bathsheba, and the Tragedy of Absalom: *A Retelling*

George Peele's Edward I: *A Retelling*

George Peele's The Old Wives' Tale: *A Retelling*

George-a-Greene: *A Retelling*

The History of King Leir: *A Retelling*

Homer's Iliad: *A Retelling in Prose*

Homer's Odyssey: *A Retelling in Prose*

J.W. Gent.'s The Valiant Scot: *A Retelling*

Jason and the Argonauts: A Retelling in Prose of Apollonius of Rhodes' Argonautica

John Ford: Eight Plays Translated into Modern English

John Ford's The Broken Heart: *A Retelling*

John Ford's The Fancies, Chaste and Noble: *A Retelling*

John Ford's The Lady's Trial: *A Retelling*

John Ford's The Lover's Melancholy: *A Retelling*

John Ford's Love's Sacrifice: *A Retelling*

John Ford's Perkin Warbeck: *A Retelling*

John Ford's The Queen: *A Retelling*

John Ford's 'Tis Pity She's a Whore: *A Retelling*

John Lyly's Campaspe: *A Retelling*

John Lyly's Endymion, The Man in the Moon: *A Retelling*

John Lyly's Galatea: *A Retelling*

John Lyly's Love's Metamorphosis: *A Retelling*

John Lyly's Midas: *A Retelling*

John Lyly's Mother Bombie: *A Retelling*

John Lyly's Sappho and Phao: *A Retelling*

John Lyly's The Woman in the Moon: *A Retelling*

John Webster's The White Devil: *A Retelling*

King Edward III: *A Retelling*

Mankind: *A Medieval Morality Play* (A Retelling)

Margaret Cavendish's The Unnatural Tragedy: *A Retelling*

The Merry Devil of Edmonton: *A Retelling*

The Summoning of Everyman: *A Medieval Morality Play* (A Retelling)

Robert Greene's Friar Bacon and Friar Bungay: *A Retelling*

The Taming of a Shrew: *A Retelling*

Tarlton's Jests: A Retelling

Thomas Middleton's A Chaste Maid in Cheapside: *A Retelling*

Thomas Middleton's Women Beware Women: *A Retelling*

Thomas Middleton and Thomas Dekker's The Roaring Girl: *A Retelling*

Thomas Middleton and William Rowley's The Changeling: *A Retelling*

The Trojan War and Its Aftermath: Four Ancient Epic Poems

Virgil's Aeneid: *A Retelling in Prose*

William Shakespeare's 5 Late Romances: Retellings in Prose

William Shakespeare's 10 Histories: Retellings in Prose

William Shakespeare's 11 Tragedies: Retellings in Prose

William Shakespeare's 12 Comedies: Retellings in Prose

William Shakespeare's 38 Plays: Retellings in Prose

William Shakespeare's 1 Henry IV, aka Henry IV, Part 1: A Retelling in Prose

William Shakespeare's 2 Henry IV, aka Henry IV, Part 2: A Retelling in Prose

William Shakespeare's 1 Henry VI, aka Henry VI, Part 1: A Retelling in Prose

William Shakespeare's 2 Henry VI, aka Henry VI, Part 2: A Retelling in Prose

William Shakespeare's 3 Henry VI, aka Henry VI, Part 3: A Retelling in Prose

William Shakespeare's All's Well that Ends Well: A Retelling in Prose

William Shakespeare's Antony and Cleopatra: A Retelling in Prose

William Shakespeare's As You Like It: A Retelling in Prose

William Shakespeare's The Comedy of Errors: A Retelling in Prose

William Shakespeare's Coriolanus: A Retelling in Prose

William Shakespeare's Cymbeline: A Retelling in Prose

William Shakespeare's Hamlet: A Retelling in Prose

William Shakespeare's Henry V: A Retelling in Prose

William Shakespeare's Henry VIII: A Retelling in Prose

William Shakespeare's Julius Caesar: A Retelling in Prose

William Shakespeare's King John: A Retelling in Prose

William Shakespeare's King Lear: A Retelling in Prose

William Shakespeare's Love's Labor's Lost: A Retelling in Prose

William Shakespeare's Macbeth: A Retelling in Prose

William Shakespeare's Measure for Measure: A Retelling in Prose

William Shakespeare's The Merchant of Venice: A Retelling in Prose

William Shakespeare's The Merry Wives of Windsor: A Retelling in Prose

William Shakespeare's A Midsummer Night's Dream: A Retelling in Prose

William Shakespeare's Much Ado About Nothing: A Retelling in Prose

William Shakespeare's Othello: A Retelling in Prose

William Shakespeare's Pericles, Prince of Tyre: A Retelling in Prose

William Shakespeare's Richard II: A Retelling in Prose

William Shakespeare's Richard III: A Retelling in Prose

William Shakespeare's Romeo and Juliet: A Retelling in Prose

William Shakespeare's The Taming of the Shrew: A Retelling in Prose

William Shakespeare's The Tempest: A Retelling in Prose

William Shakespeare's Timon of Athens: A Retelling in Prose

William Shakespeare's Titus Andronicus: A Retelling in Prose

William Shakespeare's Troilus and Cressida: A Retelling in Prose

William Shakespeare's Twelfth Night: A Retelling in Prose

William Shakespeare's The Two Gentlemen of Verona: A Retelling in Prose

William Shakespeare's The Two Noble Kinsmen: A Retelling in Prose

William Shakespeare's The Winter's Tale: A Retelling in Prose

www.ingramcontent.com/pod-product-compliance
Lightning Source LLC
Chambersburg PA
CBHW022131150726
47992CB00002B/536